A STOLEN KISS

She had last seen John Blayne, now the Earl of Wayneathe, at their great-grandfather's funeral when she was fifteen. He had been eighteen, and so handsome she could barely bring herself to look at him.

Before her now stood the very personification of masculine perfection. Tall, slender, yet broad of shoulder and muscular of leg, he wore no uniform tonight but that of town buck, with pantaloons that fit him like skin and a coat very nearly as closely tailored. She had seen no one whom the Brumwellian fashion for black coat and snowy white cravat suited so well.

Elizabeth swallowed hard and took her courage in hand. She couldn't just stand here and admire him, especially as he was doing the same to her, in a way she found unsettling.

"Well, John?" She moved toward him. "Have you forgotten your cousin?"

"I've a great many such cousins, my dear, and am indeed having trouble placing you." As he spoke he advanced upon her, wicked purpose in his eyes. Before she could quite grasp his intention, much less formulate a response, he put his arm around her waist and scooped her close to him, pressing a decidedly uncousinly kiss on her lips.

Praise for June Calvin's
Abducting Amy

"Ms. Calvin's *Abducting Amy* is perfection! A beautiful woman, powerful men, greed, lust, and thwarted love: the best of everything. I haven't read a book this good in ages. Ms. Calvin has once again managed to set the standard all romances should strive for." —Under the Covers

SIGNET

REGENCY ROMANCE
COMING IN AUGUST 2004

Poor Caroline and *Matched Pairs*
by Elizabeth Mansfield
Together for the first time in one volume, two all-time favorite love stories by Elizabeth Mansfield, "one of the enduring names in romance" (*Paperback Forum*).

0-451-21312-2

A Passionate Endeavor
by Sophia Nash
Wounded war hero Lord Huntington has sworn off marriage. But when he is cared for by charming Nurse Charlotte, she heals his injuries and his broken heart.

0-451-21270-3

To Marry a Marquess
by Teresa McCarthy
The Marquess of Drakefield knows the costs of marrying a pauper. But when his dying friend asks Drakefield to look after his widow, he must win over the wary girl—and pay the price of falling in love.

0-451-21271-1

Available wherever books are sold, or
to order call: 1-800-788-6262

THE LAST LEPRECHAUN

June Calvin

A SIGNET BOOK

SIGNET
Published by New American Library, a division of
Penguin Group (USA) Inc., 375 Hudson Street,
New York, New York 10014, U.S.A.
Penguin Books Ltd, 80 Strand,
London WC2R 0RL, England
Penguin Books Australia Ltd, 250 Camberwell Road,
Camberwell, Victoria 3124, Australia
Penguin Books Canada Ltd, 10 Alcorn Avenue,
Toronto, Ontario, Canada M4V 3B2
Penguin Books (NZ), cnr Rosedale and Airborne Roads,
Albany, Auckland 1310, New Zealand

Penguin Books Ltd, Registered Offices:
80 Strand, London WC2R 0RL, England

First published by Signet, an imprint of New American Library,
a division of Penguin Group (USA) Inc.

First Printing, July 2004
10 9 8 7 6 5 4 3 2 1

Copyright © June Calvin, 2004
All rights reserved

REGISTERED TRADEMARK—MARCA REGISTRADA

Printed in the United States of America

Without limiting the rights under copyright reserved above, no part of this publication may be reproduced, stored in or introduced into a retrieval system, or transmitted, in any form, or by any means (electronic, mechanical, photocopying, recording, or otherwise), without the prior written permission of both the copyright owner and the above publisher of this book.

PUBLISHER'S NOTE
This is a work of fiction. Names, characters, places, and incidents either are the product of the author's imagination or are used fictitiously, and any resemblance to actual persons, living or dead, business establishments, events, or locales is entirely coincidental.

BOOKS ARE AVAILABLE AT QUANTITY DISCOUNTS WHEN USED TO PROMOTE PRODUCTS OR SERVICES. FOR INFORMATION PLEASE WRITE TO PREMIUM MARKETING DIVISION, PENGUIN GROUP (USA) INC., 375 HUDSON STREET, NEW YORK, NEW YORK 10014.

If you purchased this book without a cover you should be aware that this book is stolen property. It was reported as "unsold and destroyed" to the publisher and neither the author nor the publisher has received any payment for this "stripped book."

The scanning, uploading and distribution of this book via the Internet or via any other means without the permission of the publisher is illegal and punishable by law. Please purchase only authorized electronic editions, and do not participate in or encourage electronic piracy of copyrighted materials. Your support of the author's rights is appreciated.

This book is dedicated to organizations such as the National Wildlife Foundation, The World Wildlife Fund, and the Nature Conservancy, for striving to protect the places where wild creatures still live on our crowded earth. With our help, such organizations may yet make the world safe for leprechauns!

Chapter 1

Blackmore Vale, Dorset, 1798

The faint path the two boys followed through the woods came to an abrupt halt at a steep ravine. They peered down the rocky embankment at the wildly tumbling stream they could hear churning its way downward.

"She'd never try to go down there, surely?" The younger of the two boys, John Blayne, looked at his second cousin Terrence for reassurance.

Terry examined a bush at the edge of the ravine and swallowed hard. "This bit of cloth is from the dress she is wearing, I think."

Had little Bethy tried to climb down the ravine on her stubby five-year-old legs? Had she fallen? John felt panic surge through him. He looked at Terry for guidance. "Should we go down there ourselves or go back for help?"

At that moment a sound came to them faintly above the stream's roar. It was a high, light sound, the silvery gurgle of a child laughing. Mixed with it was the musical sound of some unknown bird. They exchanged glances, and Terry plunged through the undergrowth in the direction of the sounds. John followed, then banged smartly into Terry's back when he abruptly stopped.

"Bethy Blayne, I'll tan your hide," Terry cried out in a tone in which anger mixed with relief.

At his loud declaration the sound of an animal scuttling through the undergrowth startled them, and the child who sat on a large, flat stone turned toward them. Her yellow hair glowed in the gloom of the deep woods, but the smile that lit her face quickly faded.

She jumped up, drew herself up to her full height, and put her chubby hands on her hips. "Now see what you've done! You've scared away Shamus."

Terry closed the distance between them and hoisted her up. "Shamus? Was there someone here with you? Bethy, did someone bring you here?"

John looked around carefully, a shudder passing through him at the thought that his little cousin might have been brought here by an unknown man.

"Miss Griffith brought me into the woods, then we met Papa and they said I should go back to the manor. But I got losted."

The boys exchanged embarrassed glances. Though only eight and nine, respectively, they knew enough of adult behavior to guess what this might mean.

"Your governess and Uncle Blayne went off into the woods together?" John asked.

"Yes. Papa said they had to talk about my being so naughty." Beth worried her lower lip with her teeth. "I didn't mean to be naughty, looking for Miss Griffith in the night. But I heard a funny noise and got scared. Now I am going to be caned, I 'spect."

"I hope not." Terry hugged her protectively. "But you said someone else was here with you."

"Shamus. He stayed with me and told me funny stories. He said I mustn't go down toward the water, though I wanted ever so much to see the water sprites."

"Water . . . oh, lud! You've been listening to great-grandmother's tales too much. And I suppose Shamus will have been a piskie or a brownie?" Terry tweaked her nose. Indicating that John should precede them, he started the long walk out of the woods.

THE LAST LEPRECHAUN

"Not a piskie. A leperkin. You know. The little old shoemaker."

Terry laughed and gave his sister a teasing bounce. "Silly Bethy. Leprechauns are Irish."

"I know that, but that's what he said we would call him. I do wish you hadn't frightened him away. I wanted you to meet him."

Terry gave John a wink. "Another time, perhaps. Right now, everyone on the estate and the village is out combing the fields, meadows, and woods for you."

Beth's face crumpled. "Even Papa? He's back home?"

"Home, and very angry. But likely he'll be so relieved that you are safe that he won't beat you, any more than I did. Hush, sis. Don't cry." He gave her a rough little jounce. "And if I were you, I'd not tell anyone else he was here with your governess."

Beth lifted puzzled, innocent eyes to meet her brothers'. "Why not?"

"It would just make Papa angrier."

"Why?"

Terry and John again exchanged embarrassed glances.

"Let's just say sometimes grown-ups like to keep secrets."

"Oh!" She was silent as Terry tossed her over his shoulder, hastening through the iron gate in the high stone wall that sealed the Heartwood from unwanted visitors.

A half-dozen people saw the three children as they headed across the meadow between the woods and Blayne Manor, and someone blasted a hunting horn, calling off the search. In minutes, Beth was on the steps in front of Blayne Manor, surrounded by siblings and cousins.

"Where was she?" her older sister Portia demanded.

"In the woods, conferring with a leprechaun," Terry laughed.

"In the woods! How did she get there?" This was a

concerned howl from Beth's mother. She rushed out the front door and pushed to the front of the group to pick up her daughter, holding her tightly.

"She squeezed through the gate, I guess," Terry said, rolling his eyes at John.

"A leprechaun." Portia laughed. "Silly Bethy. Bethy's seen a leprechaun! No one but Bethy could see a leprechaun outside of Ireland!" She began to laugh in that taunting, know-it-all way that older sisters have. John's brothers Roger and Peter joined her. Suddenly Beth found herself surrounded by a laughing, chanting group of children. Her mother tried to quiet them, with no success.

Terry raised his voice. "Hush, you'll bring Papa and he'll thrash her, sure. Bethy's just the age to see the fairy folk. You saw one once, didn't you, John, in Ireland?"

John frowned. "I thought so at the time."

"But at least that was in Ireland, where leprechauns belong," Portia smirked.

Beth wiggled out of her mother's arms and clutched John's jacket sleeve excitedly. "You saw a leperkin too, John? Tell them, then. Make them stop laughing."

"I . . ."

"Oh, he's long since outgrown that silliness, I'm sure," Terry said. "Now don't cry, Bethy. It was likely a little red squirrel you saw."

"It was not! It was a leperkin. Gram says . . ."

"Gram is a daft old woman, and you've listened to far too many of her stories." The new voice was deep and angry. Beth shrank from her father, who towered over her, a whip in hand. "How dare you upset the entire estate by running away from your governess and staying for hours. Not one bit of work from servants or farm hands all day long. I'll teach you to . . ."

"But Papa!" Beth shrank against her mother. "I didn't run away from Miss Griffith. I . . ."

"That will be quite enough from you!" Her father

THE LAST LEPRECHAUN

slapped her mouth and jerked her away from her mother. "Get along with you," he yelled to the group of children gathered around them. "Go back to your studies and make up for the time you have lost searching for this brat!" He started into the house.

"No," his wife shrieked, pushing her way into his path, but he thrust her back forcefully. He dragged Beth through the open manor door, past an interested group of servants, before almost crashing into a scowling old gentleman. Still tall and dignified, though virtually bald and clearly of a great age, his grandfather blocked his path.

"You will beat the child?" The deep voice, rusty with age, was pitched softly enough that none but Beth and her father could hear. "And what will you do to the governess who left her to her own devices for so long? And what caused the governess to abandon her charge?"

"I . . ."

"You and your philandering are a sore trial to me," Lord Blayne growled at his grandson. "But even worse than being an unfaithful husband is being one who fouls his own nest, as you have done with tenants' wives and daughters, with maids, and now your own daughter's governess. And then threatening to beat the child after your own behavior endangered her life. Get that shameless baggage of a governess out of here tomorrow, and never raise your hand to your daughter again!"

Geoffrey Blayne tried to stare down his grandfather, but it was beyond him. He knew he was in the wrong, and even more importantly, he knew that Lord Blayne, for all his eighty years, still firmly held the reins of power at Blayne Manor.

"Very well, Grandfather," he agreed. "She will be sent away."

"You go too. You disgust me. Shoving your poor wife like that. If Terry hadn't steadied her, she would have fallen to the ground. You are a poor excuse for a man, like your late father before you. Take yourself off to that

London townhouse I pay so dearly for, and trouble us no more. Perhaps by separating you from him, I can save Terrence from learning your ways."

"You . . . you are banishing me?"

"Don't pretend you care for your estate, or your family, or anything but your carnal pleasures. Go and enjoy them elsewhere. Don't return unless you have mended your ways."

Beth's father's face turned a deep purple, but he said nothing. After a moment more of glaring at his adversary, he stormed up the stairs, leaving Beth looking up adoringly at her great-grandfather.

"Gramp, I saw a leperkin. I did!"

"A leprechaun, is it?" The old eyes twinkled. "You saw a leprechaun in the Heartwood?"

At Beth's vigorous nod, her grandfather's eyes took on a misty look. "This will be wonderful news for your great-grandmother." The old man patted her golden head. "Go up to your Gram, love, and tell her all about it."

"May John come? He saw a leperkin once, too."

Gramp blinked in surprise and looked oddly at John, but did not question him. "By all means, you and John must go up and tell her."

John, like the others, had hovered near the door instead of dispersing as Geoffrey Blayne had ordered them to do. He came forward diffidently. "I once thought I saw one, sir, but now I am not sure."

"Ah, well, she will wish to hear anyway. How she loves to speak of the fairy folk. Go upstairs, too. You're a good boy, John. I am glad that your father let you and your brothers spend the summer with us."

John gave his great-grandfather a heartfelt hug. In truth, he and his brothers spent most summers at Blayne Manor, for his father, the Earl of Wayneathe, traveled a great deal both for pleasure and in the service of his country as a diplomat. He and his countess had little time for their children, and Wayneathe was a cold, lonely place most of the time. Only at Blayne Manor did he and his two older brothers know what it was to belong to a family. Their great-grandparents and Beth's mother were loving people who delighted in having young people around them, and Beth's father was seldom at home.

John took Beth's hand and led her up the stairs. "Tell me about your leprechaun," he invited her.

"He looked just as Gram said he would. Shorter'n me, but he looked like an old man, with a face brown as a walnut. He had on an old coat that looked like a mossy tree, green and brown both. When I first saw him, he ran from me, but when I started to go down to the water, he came out and scolded just as bad as ever Papa could, and made me sit on the rock and talk to him. Oh, John, it is ever so sad, for he says he is the last leperkin. I think he is lonely."

"Did he say what he was doing outside of Ireland?"

"He said he was bamished. Like Gramp just did to Papa. What's 'bamished,' John?"

"It means to be sent away from your home."

"Gramp just sent Papa away from home." Beth did not look saddened by this thought, so John offered her no false comfort. The two children entered their great-grandmother's room to find her sitting up, surveying them anxiously.

"Thank the good Lord you've been found, child. What was all that ruckus downstairs?"

"Papa was going to whip me, but Gramp wouldn't let him. In fact, he bamished him."

"Banished?" Gram nodded. She had no more fondness for her grandson than her husband did. "It will be more peaceful around here for a while, at least. Was it John who found you?"

John shook his head. "Terrence found her first. She was deep in the Heartwood, sitting on a rock by the ravine."

"And talking to a leperkin, Gram!"

"A leprechaun!" Her great-grandmother looked down at her, surprise and joy mingling in her expression. "You saw a leprechaun?"

Beth curved her hands into fists. "You don't believe me, do you? I thought sure you would! He looked just as you said he would. Terry laughed at me, and everyone else did too, except Gramp because he's so kind, and John because he's seen one too."

Gram put her hand to her heart. "You've seen him too, John?"

"Not this one, Gram. I think I may have seen one once on a visit to Ireland. I was about Bethy's age. The one I saw was a female, though."

"A female? In Ireland? No, no, that's not possible."

John's face flushed. Even his great-grandmother didn't believe him. "I guess I was just imagining things."

"Well, *I* wasn't!" Beth declared. "I met Shamus, and he said I reminded him of you, Gram, and he's very lonely because he's been bamished so long. He wondered why you didn't come to see him any more, so I told him about how tired you get."

"Shamus! Oh, you did see him!" Gram dragged Beth into her arms and hugged her. "I have been so worried about him since I could no longer walk far enough to visit him. He wouldn't come out for anyone else, you see."

"Why do you believe Bethy saw a leprechaun, but not me, Gram?" John asked, a little jealous.

She looked at him sadly, tears welling in her eyes. "I see I must tell the two of you a story, one I've never told the other children." She looked speculatively at Beth. "Can you keep a secret, child? Can you deny that you saw a leprechaun?

"I already tolded, Gram." Beth sighed. "Everyone laughed at me. But I did see him, so there!"

"No one believed you?" Lady Blayne looked relieved.

Beth shook her head. "Only John. But if you tell them, Gram, they'll believe."

"John, do you understand why this story must be quashed?"

"I think so, Gram." John knelt so he could look into his little cousin's bright blue eyes. "Don't you see, if you convince Terry and Roger and Peter there is a leprechaun, they'll hunt for him. And if they hunt for him, and find him, then what?"

"Maybe they'll take him back to Ireland? He says he misses it."

"Maybe they'll steal his gold. Maybe they'll put him in a cage like a creature in a traveling fair. Would he like that?"

Beth shook her head vehemently.

"Then we should keep his secret, eh?"

"Is that what you mean, Gram?"

"Yes, exactly. Now, can you keep it a secret?"

Beth thought a moment, then nodded her head. "I do believe what I saw was a little red squirrel."

Gram laughed, and John tugged Beth's golden braid affectionately. "She's a right 'un, Gram."

"Good. Then I'll tell you both a special story, something like the stories of faery I often tell to entertain you children on a long winter's night. But I know this story is true, because it happened to me, and it explains how a leprechaun came to be in a woodland in the south of England. It also explains why you can't have seen one, John, I am sorry to say."

John sat at her feet, and Beth on her lap, while Gram told them of a time when she was very young.

"As young as me, Gram?"

"Well, in a way this story begins then, for that is when I made friends with Shamus and his wife, Bedelia. I was a lonely little girl, for an Anglican minister has few friends in Ireland, and Papa didn't want me playing with the Irish."

"Why not?"

"Hush, Beth. Let's hear the story." John tugged on her braid.

"Yes, I'd better tell it quickly, for the dinner bell will ring soon. Leprechauns, of all the creatures of faery, were the friendliest to human beings, you see, which made them very vulnerable to . . ."

"What's 'vulnerbull,' Gram?"

"Easily hurt. Anyway, I liked to play alone under a little bush which was also their favorite place. If I'd been an Irish lass I'd have known not to play there, for everyone knew the faery folk favored that area, and avoided it. The leprechauns, Shamus and Bedelia, let me see them, and we talked, and soon became friends. I brought them treats. They are very fond of oat cakes with honey, other sweet things, and mushrooms. They're also fond of whiskey, but of course I never brought them any such thing as that. It would make them . . . never mind." Gram looked at the innocent eyes so intent upon her face and considered her words carefully.

"When I grew older and stronger, they grew more wary of me and wouldn't let me too near them, for fear I'd try to grab them and steal their gold. But they'd still appear occasionally and we'd talk, and I always took them treats. If they weren't about, I would leave the treats under the bush.

"When I was sixteen, your great-grandfather came to Ireland. He was in the army, and so, so handsome in his uniform! We fell in love, but our parents disapproved. His, because I was a mere vicar's daughter, with no dowry to speak of, and mine, because Gramp was a bit of a . . . well, let us just say he didn't always behave as he should, and my father thought him an immoral . . ."

"What's 'immoral,' Gram?"

John again tugged impatiently at her braid.

"Naughty. Anyway, to make a long story short, Shamus helped us to find out that we loved each other enough to defy our parents."

"Is that why he was banished?"

"Not exactly. He angered the faery queen."

"I don't see why . . ." Beth began.

"Bethy!" John tapped her mouth playfully to shush her.

"Let us just say she liked your Gramp too, and wanted him to join her in her faery kingdom. When Shamus helped prevent that, she became angry and banished him from faery. That put him in great danger. Bedelia could still come and go, but Shamus had to live on earth, without a safe retreat.

"Bedelia refused to leave him; she lived on earth too. Your great-grandfather and I married, and we made a place for them on an estate he bought in Ireland. It had a little thicket around an old tree, and we took them treats often. We made it plain that no one else was to go there, but one day a neighbor did, with his dogs—coursing hares, they were. And . . ."

Gram swallowed hard, tears standing in her eyes. "They caught Bedelia and tore her apart."

Beth began to cry in earnest, and it was several minutes before the other two could calm her.

"After that, Shamus was all alone, and when your Gramp had to return to England, I talked our little friend into coming with us. We made a special basket so he could breathe but not be seen. It's in the attic. Someday you must go up there and see if you can find it.

"Your grandfather reinforced the fence around Heartwood and locked the gates, forbidding anyone but family to go there, though it really wasn't necessary. Old superstitions and family traditions had kept the heart of our woodland the same for centuries anyway. We told no one he was here. Until today, no one but us knew. It is the only way to keep him safe. Otherwise people will be sneaking in there, trying to catch him to steal his gold."

"Does he have gold, Gram?" John's eyes widened.

"Only a little." She wagged her fingers at him. "You won't try to get it, will you?"

John shook his head emphatically.

"He has what we gave him, and some he has found from time to time. He couldn't bring his hoard from Ireland."

"Why?"

Gram shook her head. "I'm not sure."

The dinner gong sounded.

"You children must go up to the nursery. Gramp will be here to escort me to dinner soon."

"I still don't see why you say I couldn't have seen a leprechaun that time I visited Ireland," said John.

Beth bounced excitedly in her great-grandmother's lap. "That's right. And if she was a mama leperkin, maybe they could get married and make little leperkins."

Gram shook her head sadly. "Because Shamus and Bedelia were the last two. I told you, leprechauns were more trusting of human beings than other creatures of faery. They also liked being on earth better than being in faery. They liked the sun on their faces and the smells and sights of earth. They liked to work, unlike most creatures of faery, who prefer to laugh and sing and dance all the time.

"Unfortunately people, superstitious people, didn't like them. They and their dogs destroyed them when they caught them, especially if they didn't have any gold with which to bargain for their lives. Finally there were just the two, the last of their kind, and now Shamus is all alone."

In a way, John was relieved. He would not have to take any more teasing over having seen a leprechaun. "Whatever it was I saw was vicious. See where she bit me?"

"Perhaps a young fox?" Gram suggested.

"That is what Terry said when I told him, but she wasn't like any other fox I ever saw. Still, I suppose . . . Anyway, we'll keep the secret, won't we, Beth."

Beth nodded. "And I'll take Shamus treats."

Gram shook her head. "You're too young to go into the woods alone. Only in the company of the older children, do you hear? John, you can help. Since you children often take little picnics, you can help her leave something behind when the others aren't watching. Only, never, never take him whiskey, even if he asks you."

Beth opened her mouth to ask why, but John tugged on her braid again. "It makes him drunk, I'll bet, like Uncle Blayne. Too easy to catch then, huh, Gram?"

"Exactly right. You're a clever boy, John. Remember that, Beth. When you are older, perhaps you can go alone and he'll visit with you. He'll be much less lonely then. Oh, how I wish . . ."

"Dinner, my dear." Gramp entered the sitting room smiling. "You children must go up to the nursery now or you'll do without."

Two hungry children didn't like the sound of that, so with quick kisses and hugs all around, they fled up the stairs, leaving Gram and Gramp alone.

"Did you hear? He's still alive."

"Yes. Poor old fellow. Must be so lonely for him there. Wish he'd come out for me. Surely he knows I wouldn't hurt him."

"He's always feared males more than females. David, I want you to take me there again. You can carry me at least a little ways into the woods. He'd know I was there."

"I'd have to leave you there for a while. I don't like that. And you might catch a chill."

"I want to talk to him one more time before I die. John told me something today, something I don't believe, but still . . ."

"I'll hear no more talk of dying!" Lord Blayne gently assisted his wife to her feet and supported her weight on his arm. "I can't go on without you, you know that, don't you? You must stay with me."

She sighed. It was true, she knew. Her husband, though five years her senior, was as vigorous as a man half his age. She could feel her seventy-five years deep in her bones, while he still had a spring to his step and a twinkle in his eyes. But their love was so deep, she doubted either would long survive the other.

"Beth will visit him."

"Yes." Lady Blayne smiled. "She wants to now. When she is older . . ."

"Shamus will be in good hands." Lord Blayne kissed his wife warmly upon the lips, and helped her downstairs.

Chapter 2

Near the coast of Cornwall, 1817

"Please, Mrs. Longford. May I not one last time implore you . . ."

"It had better be the last time, Mavis, else I shall have you set down by the side of the road and continue by myself."

"You do not mean it. Oh, only consider what you are doing. To go near Wicked Wayneathe! You will be ruined! No decent man will want you. And all for a few trees."

"More than a few trees! An ancient and lovely wood, one of the few such stands in southern England. Moreover, if this visit resulted in men ceasing to pester me, it would be quite worth being ruined. However, Lord Wayneathe will not ruin me. He is my cousin."

"No, he isn't. He is . . ."

"I know exactly to what degree I am related to the earl, thank you!"

"Then you know it isn't close enough to allow you to go near him without ruining your reputation. Only consider. He is a man who has dedicated himself to debauchery of every kind . . ."

Elizabeth Longford reached over her head and jerked open the little trap door that allowed her to speak to her coachman. "Stop the carriage, Adams."

"Oh, no! No! I will say nothing more." Mavis McWheery put her hand over her mouth to show her sincerity.

The coachman called down to his mistress, "Why, M'um? We've but a few feet to go to be on the carriageway."

"Proceed, then." Elizabeth looked out her carriage window eagerly. She had not seen Wayneathe Abbey since the age of twelve, and remembered it as a dark, cold, Gothic pile which sent delightful shivers through the romantic heart. In the twilight of the late summer's evening, it presented a very different appearance to that treasured in her memory. Every window was ablaze with light, lanterns hung from every possible protuberance, and torches lined the carriageway, which was thronged with smart turnouts of every kind.

On the other side of the carriage Mavis voiced her mistress's thought. "He must be having a grand party."

"So he must." Elizabeth looked down at her plain black carriage dress. "I do wish that trace had not broken and cost us so much time. How very awkward, to be sure, arriving at this hour, on an evening when he is entertaining."

"We could turn around," Mavis suggested hopefully.

"And go where? There are no inns within three hours of this place. No! I have come too far to turn back now. Drive on, Adams. It is such a surprise that he is entertaining here. I had heard he seldom entertains in the abbey."

"Seldom entertains respectable folk, to be sure," Mavis muttered.

At last they reached the steps leading up to the former priory, which was the part of Wayneathe Abbey that had survived the centuries in habitable form. Suitably enlarged and updated by its succession of wealthy owners, it was one of England's most imposing private homes.

A bewigged, liveried, and impassive footman opened

THE LAST LEPRECHAUN

the door. Somewhere in the act of assisting Elizabeth out, his impassive expression gave way to one of astonishment.

"Has madam perhaps mistaken her way?"

"No, indeed. One could never mistake Wayneathe for anywhere else in England." Ignoring his obvious intention to protest further, she picked up her skirts and hastened up the steps, leaving Mavis to deal with their luggage. Ignoring the stares of other people standing about the entryway, she gave her card to the footman at the door.

"Are you expected, madam?" This man looked as astonished as the other footman had done.

"No, but . . ."

"Wait here, please. I must ask . . ." He moved quickly away to take her card to an elderly man whose impeccable evening dress marked him as a very superior servant. He stood at the foot of the grand stairway that led up to the drawing rooms. As this worthy approached her, Elizabeth realized that she had become the object of general interest, with dark masculine murmurs being offset by high female titters.

Goodness, what a fuss just because I am not in evening dress, she thought. Chin in the air, she looked neither to her right nor to her left as she waited.

The man who approached her looked familiar, but his remote features showed no corresponding recognition. "I do beg your pardon, Mrs. Longford, but this evening's entertainment is by invitation only."

"Basporth, don't you recognize me?" Elizabeth smiled encouragingly at the butler.

Surprised that she knew his name, he still maintained his freezing demeanor.

"No, madam, I do not."

"Why, I am the earl's cousin. Surely you must remember me."

"Cousin! Why, that's rich. Lookie here, gentlemen.

One of Wayneathe's *cousins* has arrived unaccompanied." The loud, slightly slurred masculine voice boomed in her ear. She glanced sideways to find a tall, corpulent man standing just behind her. She noticed that several other gentlemen, if such they were, were beginning to move in her direction. From what she saw of their female companions, their status as ladies was even more in question.

At that moment, Mavis McWheery appeared at her side.

"The luggage is unloaded, ma'am."

Her corseted, black-bombazined respectability, combined with a basilisk glare, gave the men pause, and Elizabeth gave silent thanks for her maid's austere presence. Even the butler looked at Elizabeth more closely.

"Basporth, will you not place me in a private room and give my name to Lord Wayneathe? I am sure he will recognize it, if you do not."

With one more quick look at her formidable maid, the butler reluctantly but quickly escorted her away from the accumulating cluster of men and led her upstairs to a small parlor.

"Wait here, madam," he said. "I will tell the earl that you are here." He bowed and hastened out.

Elizabeth paced back and forth for what seemed like ages, waiting for her cousin to appear. She heard the dinner bell toll, and smiled to herself. *Keeping town hours,* she thought. She felt her stomach give a rumble. They had eaten an unsatisfactory dinner some three hours earlier in a little country inn with no claims to elegance or haute cuisine.

"Mrs. Longford, I think now you see that I was right. He is not only debauched, he is also rude. He means to ignore you. We should leave this place."

"No more, Mavis. I will wait here if it be till morning. Why do you not go belowstairs and bring us both up something to eat—if you can't talk them out of sandwiches, then at least tea and toast?"

"And leave you alone in this den of iniquity? Never!"

"I haven't been molested yet. Doubtless they are all thinking more of their dinner than my virtue. Oh, Mavis, do go! I am hungry, and you are trying my patience sorely."

"Very well." With deepest reluctance, Mavis slipped from the room, scanning the hallway first for any sign of approaching seducers.

Elizabeth sighed deeply and went to the window, where she gazed down on the long south lawn that stretched to the cliffs. Mavis was living proof that devotion from a servant could be overdone. But the woman had stood by her through some trying times, and though Elizabeth often tired of her scolding, she would never let her go, and Mavis knew it.

The sound of the door softly opening, then closing, made her turn around. She drew in a deep, steadying breath as she beheld the man standing with his back to the door, scanning her insolently from head to toe, blue-green eyes gleaming with interest.

She had last seen John Blayne, now the Earl of Wayneathe, at their great-grandfather's funeral when she was fifteen. He had been eighteen, dazzling in his Queen's Dragoons uniform, and so handsome she could barely bring herself to look at him. Certainly she had hidden herself, not wanting him to look at her, for she was pudgy and had spotted skin.

At that time, he had been a beautiful youth. But before her now stood the very personification of masculine perfection. Tall, slender, yet broad of shoulder and muscular of leg, he wore no uniform tonight but that of town buck, with pantaloons that fit him like skin and a coat very nearly as closely tailored, in corbeau black. She had seen no one whom the Brumwellian fashion for black coat and snowy white cravat suited so well. His hair was almost as dark as his coat, and fell in thick curls around his high forehead. She remembered those curls from childhood. He had often been teased for them by the boys, and envied by the girls.

Elizabeth swallowed hard and took her courage in hand. She couldn't just stand here and admire him, especially as he was doing the same to her, in a way she found unsettling.

"Well, John?" She moved toward him. "Your butler was loath to admit me. He has forgotten me. Have you, too, forgotten your cousin?"

"I've a great many such cousins, my dear, and am indeed having trouble placing you. I should tell you that I don't relish second helpings, so ordinarily your arrival here uninvited would be decidedly unwelcome. Still, as I cannot recall you, perhaps . . ."

As he spoke, he advanced upon her, wicked purpose in his eyes. Before she could quite grasp his intention, much less formulate a response, he put his arm around her waist and scooped her close to him, bending to press a kiss on her lips.

Too surprised by his behavior to protest, Beth let him kiss her for a moment. But this was no cousinly kiss. There was lust in it, and she felt answering heat well up. When he tried to deepen the kiss, she pulled her head back and pressed hard against his chest with her hands, but he did not release her.

"John! This is really an improper way to greet your cousin."

"It is, indeed, but no more than I told you to expect," a loud, piercing female voice exclaimed, and John Blayne, Earl of Wayneathe, suddenly found himself under attack from an umbrella-brandishing Fury.

"Let my mistress go this instant, you villain."

John could do little else, since his hands were urgently needed to deflect the blows the large older woman was raining down upon his head and neck.

"Stop it, Mavis," Beth screamed, dodging in under her maid's pumping arm to grab her wrist. With John's help, Mavis was subdued, though her tongue continued to rain down insults until Beth slapped her into silence.

"I am sorry, Mavis," Beth said, instantly regretting her action as she saw the red print on her maid's cheek. "But you must cease. I will be safe with his lordship. You must go and get tea, as I asked you."

"Never! I will never leave you alone with this villain. Besides, there is no tea to be had. Preparations for a dinner the likes of which you never have seen have the kitchen staff in a complete uproar."

"Then you must not interfere again, or I truly, truly will let you go. Do you understand? Go sit over there, out of earshot, and do not say a word."

Mavis looked into her mistress's eyes, tears standing in her own. At last she nodded.

Beth sighed and turned to John. "I apologize to you, but she is very protective of me, you see, and . . ."

"Oh, I more than see," John growled, trying to restore his hair to some semblance of order and wincing as he ran his fingers across a knot on his scalp. "Some new way of gaining my attention. I prefer the straightforward approach. I like my women willing, so this elaborate charade is less than attractive to me."

"Charade! You really think me a lightskirt?" Beth's anger gave way to amusement. "In this dress?"

"I doubt not its inappropriateness is part of the charade. And I tire of the game, madam."

"It is no game! I am . . ."

"A real lady?" He cocked his head, considering the well-spoken woman confronting him, hands on hips. She certainly had the kind of formidable maid a true lady might employ.

"Perhaps you *are* a lady. In that case, you have mistaken your direction . . ."

"I have not mistaken my direction!"

"... and a lady should most definitely not be in this house tonight. Whichever is the case, as you are uninvited and unwilling, not to mention not properly attired for my party, you had best leave. Immediately. I'll have my servants see you out." He started for the door.

Beth ran after him, catching at his arm. "Are you going to tell me you really don't believe I am your cousin? That you aren't just being mischievous?"

Mavis ventured to mutter under her breath, "Call the wickedest man in England mischievous!"

"Your maid has the right of it. I am wicked, and this situation is putting me in a seriously dangerous mood." Abruptly he pulled her into his arms again, about to kiss her in spite of Mavis's shriek of indignation.

She struggled in his arms, refusing to let him gain access to her mouth. He kept one arm around her waist, and tried to force her chin up with the other.

"John! Didn't Basporth give you my name?"

"I suppose he did. I don't remember it, only that you claimed to be a cousin."

She stamped her foot impatiently. "Second cousin, actually. I am Elizabeth Longford." His scowl remained, only slightly relieved by curiosity. "Perhaps you will remember me as Beth Blayne."

His head recoiled as from a sharp blow. "Beth? Little Bethy? No! I don't believe it! The last time I saw you . . ."

"The last time you saw me, I was fifteen, plump to the point of being porky, and covered with spots. I am flattered you do not remember me, but I assure you . . ."

John released her chin and waved his hand impatiently to silence her. He wrinkled his forehead for a moment. "You married Longford? The vicar we used to call Longnose?"

Relief filled her. *He remembers at last. Now he will stop pretending to be a villain and become my cousin John.* She smiled. "The same."

"Why the devil did you marry that dried-up old stick?" Then he realized how he held her, and jumped back from her in horror.

"Beth! Little cousin Beth! And I have treated you like a lightskirt. But why the deuce have you come here? This is no place for you."

"It is the home of a gentleman and a hero, my cousin, my childhood friend. Why should I not come here? At any rate, you could have avoided my coming here if you had answered my letters or come to me at Blayne Manor as I asked you, no, begged you, to do."

"Letters? I . . ."

"Now don't foreswear yourself, John. I sent copies here, to your home in London, and to your solicitor. Several letters. With urgent instructions to forward them to you."

"I didn't want to read letters from Blayne Manor. Never again! I gave all my people strict orders to destroy any further communications from there."

"I take it that means Papa has written you?"

"Many times. Blaming me for every thing that has gone wrong in his life, not least of which is Terry's death." John suppressed a shudder. His uncle's cruel, vicious letters had hurt all the more for the kernel of truth in them.

"Oh, John. You couldn't have prevented Terry's death at Waterloo. You were two men in battle, and he died from enemy fire."

"But he never would have joined if he had not been burning up with jealousy over my military career. He never would have volunteered against his father's wishes after Boney got loose if it hadn't been for that."

"Which certainly wasn't your fault. It was his, and his alone, if fault it be. He wanted to serve his country."

John shuddered. The last thing he wanted to do was remember Terry and how he had died serving his country.

"All of this is neither here nor there. Why are you here, Beth? Why tonight, of all nights?"

"How could I know you were entertaining? But I am not entirely unpresentable, am I?"

That gleam that had been in his eyes earlier momentarily returned. "You are a good deal more than merely presentable."

"Thank you." Pleasure coursed through her at this slight compliment. "Then I shall change into evening dress and . . ."

"*No!* It is not a fit place for you."

Beth's perplexity grew. "But why not? It is true that one of your guests was a bit impertinent, but just because he was a little well to go . . ."

"Not all of my guests are gentlemen, and none of their female companions are ladies."

"Oh!" Beth practically bounced with delight. "Really? Lightskirts, John? Bits of muslin? Fancy pieces? *Cyprians?* Oh, I want to see them!" She started for the door to the drawing room.

"Mrs. Longford. Oh, my lord, stop her," the maid shrieked. For once, John and Mavis were in agreement. Before Beth could quite make her escape, John was upon her and dragged her back into the room.

"Good lord, Bethy, where is your sense of propriety? Didn't being married to old Longnose teach you anything?"

"I should think so! He fulminated about such women constantly, thundering about them from the pulpit as if they positively infested our little community. But I've never met one. I've always had the liveliest curiosity to see one of these fabled creatures up close."

"No sin in Whinton, eh? That's not quite how I remember it." John lifted a sardonic eyebrow.

"You know very well my father was and is a great sinner in that line, but his sins are with mundane creatures. He specializes in maids, governesses, farmers' wives . . . it is quite disgusting, for most of them haven't any choice but to give in to his demands. But I've never caught sight of a woman who would chose such a way of life, who would be so beautiful and elegant and—oh, irresistible—that men would pay for her favors, vie for them, even fight duels for them. Please let me at least take a peek at . . ."

"Absolutely not! I stand in the place of your brother here, and must protect you against that insatiable curiosity of yours. You may have changed from a dumpy child into a beautiful woman, but I see that you are as outrageously inquisitive and determined to have your way as ever."

"Oh, John, you won't even let me have at least a quick peek?"

He grinned down at her. "I remember that wheedling way of yours. It won't work with me now, though. Satisfying this sort of curiosity would damage your reputation, if not worse. It would be best if you were to leave now. I'll have Basporth escort you down the servants' stairwell so no one will see you."

"I won't! I won't go! And it has nothing to do with your Cyprians, either. I have a matter of the utmost importance to discuss with you.

"Important to whom?" His face took on a closed look. "Not to me, I assure you. The only thing important to me is pleasure, and you are seriously interfering with that this evening."

"Important to me." She smiled coaxingly. "Once upon a time, that would have mattered to you." His face remained carved in granite.

Beth shrugged. "Since that obviously isn't true anymore, be assured that it vitally concerns your pocketbook. My father . . ."

"I have it! He has sent you to throw yourself at me. Marriage to me would be one way for him to pull himself out of the River Tick. Hopes I'll try to assuage my guilty conscience by marrying Terry's sister, and paying for the privilege. Well, it's a wasted trip, Beth. Lovely as you have become, I won't marry you. I don't want a wife, you see. A wife is someone to take care of. She'd give me children." He shuddered theatrically. "Worry and woe, that is what children are. I have no time for such things. I have dedicated the rest of my life to pleasure, and won't go into parson's mousetrap for any reason."

Beth drew herself up and looked daggers at him. "He did *not* send me. Especially not to marry *you*. You are the last man on earth he would wish me to marry. Nor would I, if he did wish it. I'm determined not to marry as you. More, I'll vow!"

John lifted a skeptical eyebrow. "So you say, but you are here."

"I came about what he is doing to the estate."

"Wasting my inheritance, is he? Let him! I have enough money to throw away. I don't give a damn about the Blayne estates, no matter how many times he accused me of leading Terry to his death to gain them. You are *de trop* here, Beth. As I said before, my servants will see you are escorted safely off the estate." He moved toward the bell pull.

Chapter 3

Beth saw all her hopes about to disappear. Desperately, she pleaded with him. "Wait! You need not hear me tonight. You surely won't send us off through this dangerous countryside at this hour? We are miles from an inn, and there is no moon tonight. You couldn't be so utterly without feeling as to force me to leave on a moonless night. These roads are winding and often on the sides of steep cliffs, and . . ."

John raised his hand, commanding her silence. "Enough of your dramatics."

He paced in a small circle, once again running his hands through his hair, and once again wincing as he came in contact with the hard knots raised by Mavis's umbrella.

"Very well. I suppose you must stay the night. But join my company you may not. This improper party will last several days, and then my friends and I will disperse to our various hunts, while those females that fascinate you so will go back to . . . wherever it is their types go."

He paused, thinking things over. "Of course, most of my guests will sleep off tonight's drink until well after noon. You can rise early and leave after breakfast with no one the wiser."

"Oh, John. I knew you'd listen if I came in person. I knew it!" She threw her arms around him and bussed him soundly on the cheek.

Disdainfully he put her at arm's length. "Haven't set your sights on me, have you? Huh! I know a man-trap when I see one."

Beth drew back, fighting the urge to slap him. "That was not seduction, John. I should think you of all people would know the difference between that and a cousinly kiss. I just couldn't contain my joy that you will let me stay until tomorrow and listen to what I have to tell you."

"Listen! I didn't say I would . . ." Just then, a great shout in the hall outside, accompanied by hysterical female laughter, distracted them from their tête-à-tête. "Oh, never mind. Can't talk now. You and your maid must be gotten out of sight. I'll have Basporth conduct you to the nursery."

"The nursery? No, really, John. That is too much."

"You can lock yourself in for the night and . . ."

"Lock myself in? My goodness, what for?"

At that moment the door opened with such force it banged against the wall, and a man tumbled in with two disheveled, scantily clad females clinging to him, one on either side.

"Here you are. Party's starting without you, old man! Shabby way to treat your guests. Oh, I say. No wonder." The man shook off his companions and shoved them backwards. He swayed over to Beth and looked her up and down in the same calculating way that John had first looked at her. From this man, she disliked that look intensely.

"Delicious! Sarton told me you had an *incognita* here tonight. Private stock, Wayneathe, or will you share?"

"Desist, Melcombe. This is my cousin, my second cousin, actually, and . . ."

"Famous!" Melcombe began to laugh. "Another of your legendary cousins! Though why you need to pretend to *us,* I can't tell. You usually reserve such pranks for society's proper entertainments. Dressed as a governess, eh? Or—no—a recent widow. A poor widow." Melcombe stepped back and viewed her through fingers arranged as a picture frame, then shook his head.

"That look doesn't do a thing for me, but *chacun à son goût*. Once he tires of that game, my dove, I hope you have something a bit more revealing to put on. Then I'm your man." He chucked her under the chin.

John grabbed his arm and jerked it away from Beth. "Damn it, Melcombe, she really is my cousin. Neither you nor anyone else will lay a hand on her. Take your . . . ah . . . lady friends to the ballroom. I shall join you shortly. And say nothing to anyone else of having seen my cousin."

"Secrets? Ah, you do have some prank up your sleeves. But I fear it is too late. Several others saw her arrival. Place is buzzing with conjecture. Your real cousin, indeed! There was the redhead you foisted off on Lady Swailenthorpe. Starched-up old baggage actually believed she was your relation, let your ladybird stay right through the summer with her, even after you left the house party. Wonderful joke, that. And then there was the one you brought to the Newmarket races. Dressed as a boy, that 'cousin' was. Very pretty boy. Had some of us shaking our heads over you, don't mind telling you that. What a laugh we all had when 'he' was revealed as a she."

"Enough! You are in the presence of a lady. She is my real cousin, here on family business and accompanied by a highly respectable companion."

Melcombe looked at Mavis, standing nearby and glaring at him. "A regular gargoyle. The better to fool us, eh?" He laughed raucously.

"She's . . . never mind! You wouldn't believe me anyway." He took Melcombe's elbow and began steering him from the room. His guest struggled but was unable to prevent John from evicting him.

The two women who had followed Melcombe in did not immediately follow him back out. Instead they stared at Beth, who stared back with avid interest, taking in the details of their revealing dresses. She had heard the evening fashions of even the *ton* ladies were scanty, but surely there could be nothing more scandalous than these dresses. They left nothing to the imagination; indeed, they added to it, for the filmy bodices showed rouged nipples pressing against the tightly fitted fabric. The skirts were practically invisible, and Beth could detect no hint of petticoats. Flesh-colored tights must be all they wore underneath.

"If you plan to play the poor widow all week, dearie, I think you'll find the pickings rather lean," the buxom blonde offered. "I have a dress that'll set off your blue eyes a treat, if you would like to borrow it."

"Why help the competition?" the diminutive but shapely redhead snapped. "We can make a fortune here if we work hard. Come on, Collette. Let's join the party. Leave Lord Wayneathe to his drab." She pulled her companion through the door after the two gentlemen, leaving Beth in a silence made all the more profound because of her racing thoughts.

John! What has become of you? My beloved, gentle cousin, turned into a decadent rake.

The blonde looked back and waggled her fingers in a friendly goodbye. Beth smiled and waved back, then found herself confronted by her glaring cousin.

"Well, you've met some of them now, my dear. Curiosity satisfied? Wish to join them?"

"Which were they, John? Demi-reps? Bits of muslin? Birds of paradise? Cyprians? Oh, please don't tell me they were Cyprians."

John scowled as he shut the door. "Why not? You say the darndest things."

"Because I thought Cyprians were, well, special. Mr. Longford reserved his strongest censure for them. Thunder from on high. Fire and brimstone. I truly would have thought a Cyprian would be a bit more impressive than either of those two. I envisioned a Cleopatra type, subtly but wickedly seductive. Surely a Cyprian would not be so obvious, not to mention kind and thoughtful, as the blonde was."

"Madam," Mavis hissed. "How can you?"

"Kind and thoughtful?" John's eyes widened. "Lord, what next?"

"Well, she was. Offered to loan me a gown more to the taste of your clientele."

"*My* clientele." John's complexion darkened with anger. "I'm not running a bordello here!"

"Oh. Well, it's not clear to me just exactly what is happening."

"Naught but a bachelor party." John frowned. "Grown rather tedious, too. I'm glad that soon we men depart for the hunt, and the females depart for their assorted lairs to seek other prey."

"It seems to me *they* are the prey."

John flushed. "Willing prey, which thank the good Lord you are not. So you do agree that the locked nursery is the place for you if you insist on staying the night? Believe me, any deeper in his cups than he already is, and Melcombe would be even more difficult to convince you are a lady than he is right now. And there are one or two others even denser and more determined than he. I don't care to spend the evening fighting duels over you."

Beth sighed. "I suppose it must be the nursery, but what a dead bore! Wish I could be a fly on the wall tonight."

"I am devoutly glad that you cannot. I'll have Basporth conduct you and your maid to your rooms upstairs via the servants' stairs, and have dinner trays sent up. Do not be a fool and decide to peek through the bannisters, the way we did as children."

Beth set her mouth mulishly. "A dead bore!"

John tilted her chin up and pinched it rather painfully. "Your word on it, or I load you back in your carriage and have it escorted back to Dorset."

"Oh, very well. What time tomorrow dare I leave my prison?"

"No one will be up before noon, if then. If you breakfast at 8:00, you can be on your way long before the bleary-eyed descend the stairs."

"You won't be among the bleary-eyed, will you, John?" She looked at him hopefully. Surely, surely he didn't really participate in such outrageous matters as would occur this night under his roof.

"Yes, dear cousin, I expect I shall. With any luck, the bleariest of all. But my staff is more than competent to see to your needs and send you off."

Indignation made Beth put both hands on her hips again. "You do not mean to come down and hear me out before I leave?"

He shook his head. "I don't see the point. I no longer take on the cares and woes of others. I told you! My life is devoted to pleasure, and I doubt what you wish to foist off onto me is pleasurable."

"It might be, approached in the correct light. However, to one devoted to Bacchus and loose females, perhaps it won't." Beth thrust out her chin stubbornly. "Still, I have no intention of leaving here until we have talked. If I have to come to your room early tomorrow and toss half a dozen whores out of your bed and then sit on you to get you to listen to me, I will!"

John's nostrils flared angrily. For a moment Beth thought she had overplayed her hand, and he would return to his intention of sending her out into the night. But as he glared down at her, the expression in his eyes softened.

"That stubborn chin and those clenched fists stir my memory. Oh, yes! I remember you now, cousin Beth. Your hair is still the color of sunlight. Your eyes are still that vivid gentian blue. You have a woman's body now, but you are still the same spirited, determined Beth of my childhood!"

"Yes." She smiled timidly as he put out a forefinger to stroke her smoothly coiled braids. Those strong hands touching her did strange things to her insides. "I am still Beth."

"Beth. Grown into a beautiful woman." He swayed toward her, and cupped her cheek with his hand, then drew it away as if burned. He breathed out through his nostrils, mouth compressed. "Very well. My valet has a remedy that will put me sufficiently to rights tomorrow morning to conduct whatever business it is that we have. I will come down to you at breakfast. Now, I must bid thee goodnight." He leaned forward and pressed a chaste kiss to her cheek, then turned on his heel and marched out the door, shutting it firmly behind him.

When Beth and Mavis followed Basporth, by a circuitous route, to the nursery floor, they found several maids already frantically at work in the room. They were pulling Holland covers from furniture, dusting, and gathering linen for beds. The beds were small, and took Beth back to her childhood, when she had spent more than one night here with her sister, tucked in and watched over by her governess, while her male cousins and brother romped in the room next door.

Mavis sneezed and grumbled, and warily sat upon one of the beds. "Don't know as it will hold me, ma'am," she said, and Beth could only agree. Mavis was a tall, generously proportioned female.

"If it be agreeable, Mrs. McWheery could stay in the governess's room," Basporth offered. "It is just off here." He indicated a little closet-like room to the right of the fireplace. "I had intended it for you, madam, but . . ."

"That would be best, I think." The small beds, though far from what she was used to, presented fewer problems to Beth, with her average height and weight. The governess's bed, having been made for an adult, would make Mavis much more comfortable.

"Would madam like a fire?"

Beth shook her head. "It is quite warm here. In fact, I should like the windows opened."

Mavis shook her head disapprovingly. "The night air . . ." she began, but Beth waved her off.

"Are they such that I can raise or lower them, Basporth?"

"Not exactly, ma'am. They crank out, so that the children could open and close them without disturbing the iron bars."

"I remember now." Beth suppressed a shudder at the barred windows. As a child she had been bothered by them, always fearing a fire, and with the riotous goings on below, that ancient fear was revived. But they must have air, for the maids' efforts had stirred up dust to add to the stifling heat of the long-closed rooms.

As Basporth opened the windows, a maid arrived with a large jug of water and a basin. Beth smiled at her. "I am very grateful, as I am needful of washing off the dust of my journey. But could I trouble you for another for my maid?"

The young woman curtsied respectfully and hastened away to do her bidding.

All of this frenetic activity produced, within the space of less than an hour, a habitable room and a delicious meal, carried up and set out for them on an old gate-leg table that had been standing up against the wall only moments earlier.

Basporth then presented Beth with the key to the nursery door. He said nothing, but gave her a significant, serious look.

"Be assured that I will lock the door after you," she said, and suited action to words as the last of the maids hurried on their way.

"Well! A fine house in which respectable people have to be locked into rooms with bars on the window." Mavis stood, hands on hips, looking around her. "And in a nursery, too!"

"It is indeed a great deal worse than I ever expected of my cousin John," Beth agreed with a sigh. "Still, he has done his best to make us comfortable. Come, let us enjoy this meal before it is entirely cold."

Even as high up in the priory as they were, sounds of revelry occasionally reached their ears, and Beth had difficulty persuading Mavis that she should not stay up all night to guard her mistress's virtue. At last they settled down, and Beth had almost drifted off to sleep when she heard giggles and loud noises indicative of someone climbing the stairs.

Both masculine and feminine, the loud babble of voices approached the nursery door. They were shouting something, something vaguely familiar. Even through the walls and across the distance, she recognized some of the cries of fox-hunters. She came fully awake and realized the crowd was trying the other doors on the floor. She could hear them running through the rooms, and it sounded as if they were turning over all the furniture.

As they emerged from the room next to hers, she finally heard what they were shouting. "Hark forrard! The whore! Hunt the whore," a masculine voice shouted. "Hunt the whore!" a giggling female voice repeated.

"Pretty little cousin-whore, come out!" It was Melcombe's voice. "Hoick, hoick! Look thoroughly, everyone."

Mavis had emerged from the governess's room by this time. "Mercy save us," she cried.

"Mercy, indeed!" Fear shivered through Beth. Was John part of that shouting throng? Egging them on? Laughing at them? Was he too far gone in drink to know or even care it was she, his cousin, they were hunting?

At the sound of the knob turning, she and Mavis, with one accord, raced to the fireplace and grabbed andirons. Perhaps a few sharp blows about their heads would convince these impertinent men she was no whore. An acrid taste filled her mouth. She had only been this terrified once before in her life, the night her father announced her engagement to his gambling partner. She fought back panic as she prepared to face her foe, stalwart Mavis at her side.

Just as the mob began battering at the door, she suddenly became aware of someone else in the room. A breeze, a sound—something alerted her, and she turned toward the left corner of the fireplace. Mavis followed her line of sight and screamed. Then, being the intrepid person she was, she raced toward the man standing in the newly opened hidden doorway, andiron raised.

Chapter 4

John took the grapes from the fingers of the buxom blonde on his lap and ate them lustily, sucking on her fingers as he drew them into his mouth. She put her mouth to his, and with her tongue, attempted to recover one, leading to a tussle of tongues that was intended to arouse him. It was the sort of thing that had worked in the past, but this time, he felt only distaste. For some reason, the whole evening had gone flat, and all his efforts to immerse himself in sensual pleasure had only succeeded in boring him. It was as if he looked upon himself from some distance, watching a drunk, vulgar man make love to a drunk, vulgar woman. Deep within himself, he wished only to put even more distance between himself and the revelry going on around them.

It is Beth's appearance here tonight that has done this to me, he thought. Irritation coursed through him. *Damn the girl. Woman.* How could he have let himself be coaxed into talking to her tomorrow morning? Why was it that the brief kiss he had ambushed her with on first seeing her made the practiced lovemaking of the magnificent creature on his lap so uninspiring? His current state of mind made him very uneasy.

I never wanted to care about anyone again. And I never will. I won't even go downstairs tomorrow morning. I'll have too big a head for it, anyway. Beth will go away eventually, when she realizes I am not going to join her.

But he knew he lied to himself. He knew that she would not leave, but would wait to waylay him even if it meant exposing herself to the vulgarity of his friends and their companions. Beth, a tenacious child, had grown into an even more tenacious adult.

"What's wrong with you this evening, lord luv'ums? A little too much wine? Let's go up to your room now, shall we? Let the rest of them drink themselves into incapability. I need one more delightful ride before *you* ride off to slay birds." Barbara Butell touched his crotch suggestively. She had been his mistress an unusually long time, almost six months, and knew—surely she knew—that their time together was drawing to an end. Doubtless it was not enthusiasm for bed sport that had her so importunate, as much as a desire for a generous parting gift.

Might as well get it over with, he thought. Over half his guests had left the dinner table to disperse to other rooms, and those who remained had already begun the preliminaries to love-making. Doubtless some of them would not even make it as far as their bedrooms. *Lovemaking.* His lips lifted in a sneer. What a singularly inappropriate word for their writhings. And for his above-stairs activities, soon, with Barbara. But it was what he wanted, all he wanted from a woman.

"Of course, if you'd rather, we could give them all a show, do it right here." Barbara straddled his lap and began to fumble with the side buttons on his trouser-flap.

He stood abruptly, almost dumping her unceremoniously in the floor. "Sorry, luv," he said, catching her by the arms before she landed on her bottom. "Not in show business." He grinned to soften his refusal. "Let's find some privacy."

An unexpected sound struck his ears as he led Barbara upstairs. Rather than the usual silence pierced by masculine groans and occasional feminine giggles or shrieks, he heard a large group of people together, shouting something he could not at first make out. They were emerging from an unassigned bedroom, and when he caught up with them he saw that it had been turned inside out, the cupboards opened, the bed upended, the curtains half torn down.

"What's the meaning of this?" he shouted.

Ignoring him, one of the men started up the stairs to the next floor, shouting, "Hoick! Hoick! Whore hunt, whore hunt! Gone away! Come out, little whore-cousin! We know he's hidden you somewhere."

John dashed up the stairs to intercept the leader, not surprised to see it was Melcombe. He dragged the drunken man against him by his neck cloth. "What the devil do you think you are doing?"

"Everyone knows you are playing one of your tricks on us, pretending that beauty who came this afternoon is your cousin. We mean to find her before you can spring the joke." Melcombe waved his hands. "No sense in you having two delectable blondes. Gonna wager for her, or share her around if her price is reasonable."

James Hodkins seconded the plan. "If you've any objections, we'll just tie you up, eh, fellows?"

A shout of gleeful agreement went up. Someone began pulling off John's already disheveled neck cloth for the purpose.

John let go of Melcombe's tie to grasp his own tightly. He laughed. "So you've smoked out my plan. No, I have no objections. The chit turned out to be a dead bore. Find her if you can, but don't tear up my house doing it. She's easily found, once you reach the right room. No need to disarrange the furniture. Come, Barbara, we have lost too much time already." He pulled her to him, leering lasciviously at her.

"Oh, can we not join the hunt?" Barbara pouted.

"Certainly not. I didn't hire you go galloping around my house looking for stray females." His fingers closed about her wrist, and he dragged her back down the stairs. She didn't struggle, and when they entered his bedroom, she cuddled against him. He urged her onto his bed. Then, to her astonishment, he jerked open a cupboard and yanked out a handful of neck cloths. He quickly tied her up, hand and foot. She protested, "You know I don't go for the rough stuff, not even for extra money."

"No rough stuff, Babs. Don't be afraid. I just need you to be quiet for a little while." He then gagged her and tied her hands to one of the bedposts for good measure.

Hastening down the hall, which mercifully was empty, he entered a linen closet. Shoving a large cupboard away from the wall, he activated a hidden switch, and a door opened inward onto some steep stairs. He started up them, then swore softly as he realized how dark they were. He retreated to grab a pair of candles from a wall sconce. His heart raced as he hastened up the steep stairs. *I've got to be in time. Should have brought pistols in case . . . no, no time to go back.*

Beth threw herself after Mavis, managing to knock up her elbow just as she struck at John, who raised his right arm to shield his head. This tilted the candle in that hand, dripping hot wax on his forehead. Then Mavis's aborted but still sharp blow hit his shoulder, nearly knocking him down.

"Stop that, damn it," he bellowed. "That's no umbrella! You could kill me!" He struggled to regain his footing.

"Mavis, stop!" Beth screamed, as her maid drew back her arm for another blow.

"He's one of them. The worst. He . . ."

"No. He's come to save us. Go get the candles from the bedside. Hurry, do. That door will give way in an instant."

"No time," John said, pushing Beth past him into the

hidden stairwell. "Come now, Mrs. McWheery, or stay behind to face them."

"I'll not let you have my mistress so easily." Mavis pushed her way past him, and he shut the secret door just as he heard the door to the nursery begin to splinter.

"Quickly, but carefully. The steps are steep." John handed one of the candles to Beth to light her way.

"I've been down these stairs in the dark, remember?" She looked back up at him, a saucy grin on her face. "On a dare by you and Terry."

"No time for memory lane. Watch where you are going," he growled.

A few minutes' descent brought them to the linen closet, but John did not let them enter it. Instead, he indicated they should continue down the stairs. "There's a small room at the bottom. You remember how to get in, Beth?"

She nodded. "Hope it's not filled with spiders."

"No spiders would dare dwell in any corner of Basporth's domain. Wait just a moment." Filling his arms from the linen press, he handed blankets and sheets to the two women.

"Here, you'd best take some more of these, too," he added, ruthlessly raiding his housekeeper's cache of beeswax candles. "I'll get you out when things calm down."

"They'd better calm down soon." Mavis's voice quivered. "I can't stand the dark."

"I'll be back long before these run out." He grabbed a few more for good measure. "But I'm afraid you may have to bed down there for a few hours."

Mavis complained all the way down, and John grinned as he listened to Beth trying alternately to pacify and to intimidate her into shutting up. He rubbed his shoulder ruefully. It would be sore tomorrow! Both women still carried their andirons. He'd have to remember not to startle them when he went down to the priest's hole later.

Once they had disappeared down the secret stairway, he slipped through the opening behind the linen chest, shut the door to the stairwell, and slid the chest back into place. Then he hastened to his bedroom, where he untied Barbara.

She complained almost as heartily as Mavis, but John could not exactly blame her. "Hush, Babs. I'll put an extra 100 guineas in your check tomorrow, if you do as I ask."

At last she calmed down enough for him to explain. "I must stop the destruction of my house by this stupid mob. I'm going to round up some servants and shotguns. A good many of my guests may be sporting buckshot by tomorrow. You are not to tell anyone I tied you up, or left you for a while. Anyone, do you hear me? Ever! As far as they are to know, I was making love to you when I heard the sound of wood splintering and decided to get my servants and stop them."

Barbara nodded. "I've got it. Some secret place, a priest's hole. You want it to remain a secret. That's where you've hidden her. But you really don't want them to find her? It isn't all a part of the entertainment?"

"No. She really is my cousin. Anyone who hurts her is a dead man."

Barbara dropped back against the sheets, arranging her body seductively. "You are terrifying when you look like that. And so very attractive, too. Will you return to me when order is restored, luv'ums?"

John shrugged. "Perhaps. Your purse won't suffer either way."

"You really do think it's only about money, don't you?" The buxom blonde scowled at him, then turned over on her side. "Don't bother waking me. I need my beauty sleep."

John felt like a captain again, organizing his senior male servants and arming them with shotguns from the gun room. "I'll shoot over their heads once for warning," he told them. "If any of them persist, hand me another gun, Basporth, and I'll put a round of shot in their legs. That should end it, but if not, if any of you have to fire, remember to aim low. Some of them may have to be carried out of here, but I would prefer that there not be any fatalities."

They caught the mob in the act of tearing up the room Beth and Mavis had been in. Hodkins, one of the more enterprising and sober of the group, was tapping along the fireplace trim, guessing there must be a secret door. "Priest's hole, that's where he's taken her. Priest's hole. That's the joke. Whore in the priest hole!"

The others started toward the wall, eager to join the search, when John fired the first shotgun blast at the ceiling. Plaster rained down upon the group, and the women screamed.

After he had overcome his astonishment, Hodkins laughed. "Hah! 'Bout to discover your secret, aren't we. You're beaten, Wayneathe. What was the wager, by the way?"

"There was no wager," John said, taking the second gun from his butler. "And there is no more house party. You will all cease and desist, or you will be carried out of here full of buckshot."

The ladies shrieked and started separating themselves from the men. They rushed toward the door, which would have carried John and his men backwards.

"Stop, ladies. Stand over there by the window. You'll be out of danger there." John motioned with the gun. The women moved into the opposite corner of the room, crouching beneath the farthest window.

"You're jesting," Melcombe said, wagging that knowing finger. "You wouldn't shoot your friends."

"No, I wouldn't. But my friends wouldn't tear up my home. I have no friends here, I think."

As he spoke the words, he realized, almost with a sense of relief, that he spoke the truth.

"Now, Melcombe, you are the closest, and will be the worst wounded if I fire. Do you wish to persist, or to go to your room, pack, and leave? This party is over."

For a moment it looked as if Melcombe would resist, but John leveled the gun at his legs, and awareness of danger at last drove out the fatuity of drunkenness. "You really mean for us to leave now? Dead of night?"

"As soon as you can be packed and away. An hour at the latest."

Grumbling spread among the men, and for a moment John feared he might have to actually put birdshot in a few of them.

But Hodkins, like Melcombe, had begun to grasp John's intense anger. "Fine way to end a house party."

"I know. You can all dine out on the story for months. Now, one at a time, leave the room. Your servants are being awakened as we speak. You will see my armed servants in the hall. They will supervise your packing and removal. Ladies, this means you, too."

John took a brace of candelabra and some more candles down the secret stairs with him. Cautiously he approached the door to the priest's hole. He called out before venturing to open it, but in spite of that precaution, Mrs. McWheery stood guard at one side, arms upraised, ready to break the head of anyone who entered. Beth stood on the other side of the door, just as prepared to do damage.

"Thank heavens," Beth said, as both women lowered their arms. "We heard the shot. Were you injured?" She examined the burn marks on his forehead.

"Not by them. You and your maid take the honors for that." He grinned at her. "It just took a round of buckshot to focus their attention. The servants are escorting them from the grounds now."

"You fired on your own guests and are now making them leave at gunpoint?" Beth's eyes flashed with merriment.

"It will doubtless become known as the third battle of Wayneathe Abbey." John laughed. He held out the candelabra and the candles, which Mavis took with a grateful murmur.

"Thank goodness for those. Mavis is afraid of very little, but total darkness . . ."

"It can be unnerving to anyone," John said kindly, noting Mavis's embarrassed posture. "Now, I need the two of you to stay here a little while, until I am quite sure the castle has been rid of its unwanted guests. Get some rest if you can. I will fetch you when all is safe."

It took longer than John had expected before the last of his still-drunk, angry guests had been routed. Barbara drove off with one of them, a generous check tucked in her cleavage. Melcombe had the nerve to ask if this meant the invitation to join John at his lodge in Scotland was off.

"You don't really want to be walking fields with me with a gun in my hand any time soon," John assured his now-unwelcome guest. Melcombe retreated quickly at the look on his host's face, and scrambled into his carriage.

Dawn tinged the sky by the time he could once again make the trip down to the priest's hole. His cautious call went unanswered, so he entered gingerly. His precautions were unnecessary. In the dim light of guttering candles he saw both women sound asleep, wrapped up in the blankets and sheets he had provided.

As he looked at Beth's sleeping face, something tender and warm washed through him. Something very unwelcome. He frowned and backed off. He had gone to a great deal of trouble for her tonight, but only because she was his kinswoman, which meant his honor was involved. Never, never, would he let himself care for her or for any other human being.

Jaw firm, he bent down to shake her awake. She started, looking momentarily frightened, then deeply pleased to see him. He straightened up and snapped, "Time to get up. The battle of Wayneathe Abbey is won. I'm glad to see you got some sleep. My servants will see to your breakfast and then you can be on your way. If you will excuse me now, I am exhausted, and will be turning in. I expect to sleep all day."

Beth sat up in a swirl of blankets. "Get your rest, by all means. But I am not leaving until we have talked."

"Damn you, Beth, I . . ."

"How dare you speak to my mistress that way?" Mavis leaped up from her bedding. "You have spent too much time in low company."

John ran his hands through his hair, wincing when he once again accidentally brushed the knots Mavis had raised with her umbrella.

"I beg you pardon, Mrs. McWheery, Beth. What I meant to say was . . . No, never mind. I will meet you in the breakfast room in thirty minutes. You may speak your piece there, and then be on your way."

Chapter 5

Beth and Mavis wearily climbed the stairs from the priest's hole. In the nursery they found that considerable damage had been done to the room, and their belongings were scattered everywhere. In a great panic Beth searched for the one thing she would never be able to replace, her portfolio, and at last found it beneath an overturned bed. With a sigh of relief, she helped Mavis round up the rest of their possessions, in spite of the maid's insistence that it was her job. Then they each went to seek their breakfasts, Beth carrying the precious portfolio with her. As she descended the stairs, she saw sleepy servants struggling everywhere to set the messy priory to rights. It was clear that more than mere housekeeping would be required, and Beth wondered if John cared enough about Wayneathe Abbey to hire the carpenters and plasterers necessary to restore it.

A footman directed her to a pleasant little breakfast room, which she found empty. Irritated and worried that John might be going to stand her up, she nevertheless eagerly accepted a large helping from the generous offerings on the side table. Just as she was beginning to eat, John came in, clearly showing the results of a valet's ministrations, but looking no less cross than he had when he awakened her.

John grimaced when he saw her full plate. He

eschewed the sideboard, settling down beside her with nothing but a cup of coffee, filled for him by the waiting footman.

"Now, I don't wish to rush you, but . . ."

"Yes, you do." She grinned pertly at him. "If you are not going to eat, perhaps your footman could be spared. I know there is plenty for him to do elsewhere in the house."

John signaled the man to go, then leaned his head on both hands and looked up at her from under frowning eyebrows. "I am waiting."

"Father is cutting down the woods."

John sat there, his expression not altering. "Harvesting timber is what one does in a wooded area. It is a large part of the income of the estate."

"He intends to cut all of them, including the Heartwood, John."

He sighed. "I am aware of what you meant by *the woods*."

Beth felt as deflated as a hot-air balloon once the burner had been turned off. "You don't care that father is destroying a woods that our family has protected for seven hundred years? Not just cutting them down, John, but grubbing out the stumps. No pollarding, no coppicing. Complete annihilation."

He shrugged. "I make it a point to care as little as I can about anything."

"When did you become such a care-for-nothing, John? And why?" Sadness washed through Beth as she realized what a bleak person he had become.

"Never mind that," he snarled. "Leave me be, Beth."

"But those woods are part of the entail," she wailed. "He is stealing your inheritance."

"I don't need the money, Beth. Your father obviously does."

"He doesn't need it, not really. It is just more to waste on gambling. Why should the Heartwood be sacrificed for such an ignoble cause?"

"I doubt it's just about money. It's about Terry." John leaned back in his chair and closed his eyes. "He blames me for Terry's death. I shouldn't doubt he's cutting them down to spite me. And nothing I could say to him would change his mind. He despises me. A protest from me would only give him pleasure."

"I know. But that doesn't make it right. The law is on your side, if only you will . . ."

"I don't need the income from those woods, or indeed from any of his estates. Don't want the title, don't want any of it."

"Ironic, since that is what particularly sticks in father's craw—the Blayne barony will be subsumed under the Wayneathe earldom, though your title is younger and comes from the successes of your grandfather and father."

John opened his eyes slightly, and she could see some emotion there, deep and painful, but could not determine what it was. "I can't change that. He is grief-stricken—half mad with it, I shouldn't wonder. Let him cut down the woods if it will make him feel better." He started to rise.

She put her hand on his arm. "Don't you care about them at all? About how much Gramp and Gram cherished them? About how Gram charged all of us children, almost with her dying breath, to protect them and . . . and the creatures that live in them? They are possibly the oldest woods in England. Some of those trees go back to before the Roman Conquest. The woods were listed in the Domesday Book. Don't you think that heritage is worth preserving? Gramp did. It's why he kept the prohibition against harvesting the Heartwood timber in the entail."

"Gram had a great deal to do with that, and you know she wasn't protecting the woods, poor, dear, daft woman." John's expression softened as he thought of their great-grandparents. They had helped provide the stability and love he never had from his own father—much less his grandfather, the consummate warrior and diplomat who had started their branch of the family along its way to a lofty title. But still he rose from his seat and tossed down his napkin, signifying that the interview was over.

Beth jumped up, tears in her eyes. "How can you call her daft?"

"Now, Beth, you know she really believed all those delightful stories she told us. At the end, anyway. She doubtless started telling tales about fairies, goblins, ghosts, piskies, and brownies as entertainment for the children of the family, but by the time she died she believed every one of them, and made us swear to do so too."

"Which we did."

"Out of respect, yes, and love."

"Then don't you think, out of respect and love, you ought to keep that pledge?"

"I was fully aware that it was a promise made to please, to pacify—not one made to a rational being for a rational reason."

"You never meant it, then. You never meant it when you promised to keep the Heartwood safe?"

"It never occurred to me that I would have the power to do so."

"Still, you promised. Does your word mean nothing?"

He winced, but held firm. "Not in this instance."

"John, before you leave, let me show you something?" Beth jumped up and dashed across the room to where she had propped up her portfolio."

"What is it?" John asked, eyeing it warily.

"Drawings I've made in the woods. We had such good times there. Do you remember that? Do you remember how beautiful it is there? If you don't care about the money, if you can't believe in the creatures of faery, can't you care about all the wild things that live there? I've made a study of the place. I've become a considerable

THE LAST LEPRECHAUN

natural historian, in point of fact. I know there are many animals, plants, and insects living there which are either very rare or not found at all elsewhere in Britain. Where will they go if the woods are cut down?"

John sighed wearily. "I don't know. And I'm sorry. Sorry for their destruction, and for your sorrow. But I won't confront a man maddened by the loss of his son, and try to tell him what to do with his property, just to save insects and birds."

"Maddened. Alas, that is too true. Madder than you guess. Still, I thought if somehow you could make peace with him, he would stop this frenzy of destruction."

"Make peace with your father? Only by dying and making Terry live again in my place. Which I wish I could do." The haunted, terrible look on John's face told Beth the source of the bleak expression that she had seen in his eyes more than once in the last few hours. She wanted to put her arms around him and comfort him. She propped the portfolio back against the wall and moved toward him, arms outstretched.

"It wasn't your fault."

"No." He retreated, his expression closed, his posture stiff, clearly not a man to allow himself to be comforted.

"You say no, but you don't seem to believe it. You'll have to forgive yourself. Then perhaps you can convince him to forgive you."

He shrugged. "If it wasn't my fault, there's nothing to forgive, is there? Go away, Beth. Let me be."

Beth took a deep breath. Her heart pounded as she nerved herself to say what she had hoped to avoid saying.

"What if I told you he is tearing down the woods not just for the timber, but to get at Shamus."

"Shamus?"

"Now, don't tell me you have forgotten Shamus?"

John's brow wrinkled. "The leprechaun?"

Beth nodded, holding her breath.

"Ah, no. He really has gone mad, then."

"You called Gram daft, and think father mad. Yet, once you saw a leprechaun. You believed in them then."

"I thought I did. I was only six at the time. And if you don't remember, it was Gram herself who told me I could not possibly have done so."

"You believed in them when you were much older than that. Remember when we took Gram's little box into the woods for her, just before she died?"

"I did it for the same reason I made those promises — because I loved her and she was so urgent about it. Something about the leprechaun needing the gold for his protection."

Disillusionment made Beth's shoulders sag. "So you pretended to believe? For all those years? You humored me, too, then, as well as grandmother, for you used to go with me to take the little baskets of oatcakes and sweet biscuits."

"It wasn't always pretense. I was an imaginative child, as were you. But now . . . Ah, Beth, I don't believe in *anything* now, least of all leprechauns."

Beth's eyes widened in shock. "Don't believe in . . ."

"Anything. Not in God or the devil, heaven or hell. Nothing except sensation. The here and now. Wine, women, a fast horse flying over a dangerous fence. Anything that gives me physical pleasure. God? Ah, if I believed there were a God, I'd hate Him. After the carnage I've seen? Good men dying, their flesh shredded, pain unrelieved. Men and horses dying of thirst in the hot sun after a battle while scroungers tear off their clothes."

His eyes took on a fierce glare. "We couldn't get men or wagons in to collect the injured, but the scroungers could marshal an army of vultures to strip them clean, and kill them if they had enough life left in them to object. Where was God then? Where was He in the tents in which the wounded were carved up in the guise of treatment? Ah! I wish I believed in faery. I'd sooner live there than on this earth! But there is nothing, Beth. Nothing."

Beth knew she was looking into the eyes of a man who had seen hell on earth. Again that urge to comfort him came over her, but the ferocity of his expression kept her at bay. She sought desperately for something to say that might change his mind, but all she could think of would sound like platitudes to him. She feared she would only further alienate him, so she stood silent, wringing her hands.

"Chance, Beth. It is all chance. It was through no virtue or cleverness that I lived while Terry took a shot in the gut right beside me. He stood between me and the shooter. If not for him . . ."

"It wasn't your fault."

John didn't see her, or even hear her, it seemed to Beth. His eyes stared out over a landscape remembered, horror darkening his features.

"He took so long to die. The lucky ones died instantly. I held him in my arms. To hell with the battle! I held him and watched him suffer, heard him moan in anguish. Watched him die. Then picked up my gun and sword and killed as many Frenchies as I could, like a devil. I became a devil! And then it was over. Over! Suddenly, after all those years of soldiering, it ended in the blood-soaked fields of Belgium. I could come home to my family. I longed for my mother's embrace, my brothers' eager welcomes. If my father ever loved me, I never knew of it, but he died while I was away soldiering. That was a matter of indifference to me, but when I disembarked my ship only to learn that . . ." His voice broke. He turned away.

Beth knew, of course, about his two brothers' and his mother's deaths. She put her hand on his arm, but he shook it off and turned on her.

"In a fire!" he shouted. "Burned alive while waiting at an inn at Dover for my ship to come in. Came to meet me because they were eager to see me again. All those years of risk, of watching my friends die around me while I survived without a scratch, and I return to find my entire family gone. I alone survive. But for how long? For what purpose? What horrible death awaits me? What compassionate God protects me? Why didn't He protect them? Because there is no God, nor meaning in the world. I lived, they died, because it's all chance.

"No! I don't believe in your leprechaun. I am surprised that you still believe in such nonsense, and astonished to hear that your father does, but it is none of my concern." He slashed his right hand downward, hitting his left palm. "I believe in nothing but pleasure. It would not give me pleasure to confront your father, I assure you. I have had a surfeit of sexual pleasure, so now I go off to hunt, to feel the cool moist breezes of fall upon my face, to listen for the whirr of wings, to bring down my prey and eat it, savoring every bite. Such is what I want, what I believe in. There is no such thing as faery, Beth, or God. There is only sensation, and I intend to enjoy as many of the pleasurable ones as I can until the oblivion of death engulfs me."

"Then there is no such thing as right or wrong?"

"I . . ." John hesitated. "It's only logical. If there is no God, then what makes one thing right and another wrong?"

Beth cocked her head. "True enough. I see I have been living my life quite stupidly. I, for instance have not had a surfeit of pleasure of any sort. I have been the dutiful daughter of a cruel father, the chaste wife of a dull man. Since you have had a surfeit of such pleasure as he could never provide me, perhaps Mr. Melcombe could supply it. He is a handsome man, and took some interest in me last night. Has he left? If not, in which room is he staying?" She started for the door, looking expectantly back over her shoulder.

John stared at her as if she had suddenly sprouted horns and a tail. "You'll do no such thing. What insanity is this?" He crossed the room and grabbed her arm, hard, whirling her around to face him.

"Oh! Perhaps you'd accommodate me, instead. I quite enjoyed that kiss you gave me last night when you thought I was a demi-mondaine." She pressed herself against him, lifting her head and offering him her lips.

"A demi-mondaine is what you'll become at this rate!" An odd glimmer in his eyes, John held her against him for a long moment. Then he thrust her away. "Leave off this nonsense. You are just trying to shock me."

"True. I'm trying to make you see how wrong you are. And you know it. There *is* right and wrong. If there's not, why shouldn't I seek out a companion, numbers of them, for my bed?"

"I was speaking for myself only."

"But what's sauce for the gander . . ." She again threw herself into his arms. At his growl of disapproval, she laughed. "Think of what a world it would be if all believed as you do."

"Oh, I agree it is well enough for the lower orders and women to believe in God and virtue and heaven and hell. Keeps them performing their proper roles in society." He succeeded in propelling her to arm's length and held her there.

"That is the most hypocritical thing I have ever heard anyone say. No! I won't have it. If you feel that the only thing worth doing is seeking pleasure, then why shouldn't everyone follow that philosophy?"

He seemed unable to reply. Eyes narrowed, he stood silent. Beth felt she had reached him, or at least given him some food for thought.

"Please, John. It is your duty to preserve the heritage of the Blaynes, and that includes the Heartwood. Come back to Whinton with me and talk to Papa, threaten legal action, threaten to lock him up, do whatever it takes to stop the wanton destruction of the Heartwood."

"No!" He shook her hard. "You aren't listening to me! I want nothing to do with this. Go home!"

Beth felt momentarily dizzy from his violence. She

swayed on her feet. Looking into his set countenance, she knew her errand had been in vain. "I see you are my father's true heir, in every way. Atheist and libertine, and assaulter of women." She turned and walked from the room. She had made it halfway up the first flight of stairs when John called to her.

"Wait!" He took the steps two at a time. "You mentioned that your father was cruel. Is he abusing you or your mother?"

"Both, intermittently, when he is not too drunk for us to escape. But that doesn't concern you, does it? You care for nobody."

A surge of fear tore through John, for he knew his self-created emotional armor had been pierced after all. He found he could not remain as indifferent as he wished.

"Yes, it does concern me. I am the head of the family, after all. I . . . I beg your pardon for shaking you so. I am not a monster, Beth. To prove it, I shall give you and your mother sanctuary. Go home, get her, and take her to my estate in Kent. I'll send some footmen who are former members of my troop to escort you. I'll see a guard is set to prevent him from carrying her off or threatening you. If he makes the attempt, I shall sue him for the value of the Blayne timber. That should make him behave. In the next season, you can look about you for a second husband, and . . ."

"Never!" She said it so emphatically it made him jump. "Whatever I do, I will never marry again."

John frowned as at some unknown species of animal. "Why? You are young, and must want a husband, family? Women do."

"This one doesn't."

"Don't tell me old Longnose beat you or abused you?"

"He was a civilized man, kind as the world measures such things. But one marriage is quite enough for me. Nor do I wish you to take me to your Kent estate. I want to spend my life in Whinton, studying the flora and fauna of the Heartwood and helping the poverty-stricken people of the area who have been so hurt by my father's negligence of his estate."

John frowned. "You truly do not wish to remarry?"

She shook her head emphatically.

"Well, that takes away my theory about why you are really here, why you are so persistent in trying to draw me into your world again."

She spoke through gritted teeth. "The truest words I ever spoke! You conceited jack— You really thought I had come here to call myself to your attention."

The uncompleted insult made the color rise in John's cheeks, and he felt called upon to defend himself.

"After all, I am one of England's most eligible bachelors. It seems everyone thinks I should have a wife, and soon, to carry on the line. I have to fend marriageable females off with as much skill as I ever used to escape capture in battle."

"Well, you can rid yourself of that fear. I am the last woman to try to lure any man into marriage, particularly you!"

Nettled, John could not but ask, "Why particularly me?"

"Because I have seen the pain a libertine husband causes his wife and family! Though I do think you should fall in love and marry. If you truly loved her, the love of a good woman might save . . ."

"Whom I would doubtless have the pleasure of watching die in childbirth!"

Beth shook her head. "You say you came through the war unscathed, but you didn't. Oh, John, you are grievously wounded. In here." She laid her hand over her heart. "I can certainly understand why, but I do not think healing will come by this reckless dissipation you call pleasure."

"I don't want healing, I want to forget. Now go away. You remind me of happier times, times gone never to return."

Beth unexpectedly chuckled, an ironic rather than an amused sound. "I thought Father hated you as much as it was possible to do. But he will be even more angry with you when he learns you do not plan to marry and continue the line."

"Damn the line. Do you hear me, Beth? I don't want to bring children into the world to suffer. The fewer born, the better, and I'll not add my flesh and blood to those whom capricious fortune can shred and bleed and burn and . . ." He turned away, his voice breaking. "Get out! Go! I have already ordered my servants to bring your carriage around. Get your maid and get out of here before I throw you bodily into the carriage."

Silence reigned for a long, long moment.

"I will pray for you, John. You may have stopped believing in God, but He hasn't stopped believing in you."

"*Go!*"

He turned his head around, his face as savage as his voice. Alarmed, Beth hastened to obey. She found her maid ready, her trunks packed. John's servants had already loaded her baggage on her carriage. Heart heavy, she climbed in and began the journey back to Blackmore Vale.

Chapter 6

John had intended to sleep for at least twenty-four hours, but awoke after three with a splitting headache and a deep sense of unease. Was it guilt? He refused to feel guilt. It was one of the emotions he had determined to give up, along with love. So he rose and dressed himself. He had told his weary servants to do the least amount necessary to set the house to rights and then go to bed, as most of them had been up all night. When Basporth had protested, he had insisted.

"I will doubtless sleep till morning. No need for lunch or dinner. If I awake, I can make my own way to the kitchen." He had been forced to be quite insistent, as Basporth could barely contain his distress about the state of the priory. The dedicated butler would doubtless have kept everyone, including himself, working until they dropped, otherwise.

Thus, the priory was unusually quiet as he prowled the halls, upstairs and down, appalled at the depredations of the night before. How had he managed to collect such a worthless, drunken mob? How had he managed to enjoy their company?

The answer to the latter question lay in the occasional empty bottle of wine he found here and there in the wrecked bedrooms and under tables and banquets in the halls. As for how he had collected such a low group, he knew it was money liberally spent for low pastimes that attracted them. He had avoided anyone who might be considered a true friend since his return to England. A true friend might be as appalled at the state of his mind as Beth. A true friend would, in attempting to help him, touch his raw wounds. The drunken mob he had run off last night had touched no wounds, made no demands except that he enjoy the same mindless pleasures they sought.

He knew as he looked about the priory that there needed to be extensive repairs and redecorating. He would forego the redecorating. After all, his next drunken party would result in much the same kind of damage. But to his surprise, he found he could not so easily dismiss the broken doorframes, shattered plaster, and broken furniture. His last stop was the nursery room, where he looked at the shotgun damage on the ceiling and pondered what might have happened if he had not arrived in time to rescue Beth from his so-called friends. A shudder went through him. His notion of pleasure did not include rape, and suddenly he knew he would not ever again associate with the men he had routed from her room.

Well, I managed to send the drunken sots on their way, he thought with some satisfaction. He wondered briefly with whom he would hunt and carouse now, but knew that there was always a surfeit of such types around. Perhaps he would just go to Scotland alone, though. Spend a little quiet time there, just he and his dog and his gun. It had a definite appeal.

There would be no quiet times at the priory for a while, for he would order repairs to be made while he was gone. Somehow he could not just let his ancient home remain in such condition.

The next day he sought out Basporth, and gave him a list of repairs to be made.

"Any other damage you discover which I missed, you are authorized to repair also. I have ordered my carriage,

THE LAST LEPRECHAUN

and am away to Scotland. I put all in your competent hands."

Their conference took place in the breakfast room. John had insisted the elderly butler join him for breakfast. Basporth made notes as he ate, and it seemed to John the old retainer's face looked less grim than it had in some time. *He approves of my plans,* John thought, grimacing internally at how long it had been since he had done anything his worthy family retainer approved of.

As John started to leave, Basporth drew his attention to the large portfolio propped up against the wall.

"Mrs. Longford appears to have left something behind, my lord. Shall I send it to her?"

"Yes, I suppose so." John bent to pick it up. It was heavy, bulging with what he supposed must be drawings of the Heartwood, drawings she had hoped would convince him to enter the fray against his uncle. He glanced briefly inside, ruffling through the papers, and noted some highly detailed, sophisticated drawings. He hadn't realized Beth had become such an accomplished artist. Of course, he hadn't realized a great many things about her, including the fact that she had grown into a beauty with a wilful and somewhat unconventional turn of mind.

"Never mind," he told Basporth, glancing out the window at the rain-swept view. "I'll take it with me to look at in the carriage. It's too filthy a day to ride; it will give me something to do. I can send it to her from Scotland."

"Very good, my lord. I will place it in the carriage, then."

"Nonsense. I can carry a damned portfolio. You look done in, Basporth. This entertainment was far from a sinecure for you and the servants. You get some rest, do you hear?"

Very much on his dignity, Basporth drew himself up. "If my lord thinks I am too old to serve . . ."

"I couldn't do without you. Don't you dare retire! It's

because I want you around for years to come that I insist you take care of yourself.

Basporth bowed, mollified, and escorted his master out onto the front portico. John placed the portfolio in the carriage and followed it with reluctance. Ordinarily he would ride most of the way; saddle horses were already arranged along the route, and one was being led by a groom so he could ride as soon as the rain let up.

He hated being confined in a closed carriage. Above all, he hated being confined with people who annoyed him, which included his valet. For that reason he had sent his valet on ahead, to prepare for John and several guests, guests who would never arrive.

This bachelor party had seemed such a good idea at the time. Wine, women, sensual pleasures. He was exhausted and found that looking back on the wild orgies of the past week gave him no pleasure, even omitting that last, disastrous night. He wondered if he had really enjoyed any of it.

So, I am dedicated to seeking pleasure. Whence shall I find it, if such revels cease to amuse? He stared moodily out the window. Beth's suggestion that she might as well follow his example, her unsubtle insinuation that his philosophy would do great harm if followed by most people, had burrowed into his brain box like a burr in his favorite collie's coat. Worst of all was the comparison she had made between him and her rakehell father.

Snippets of their conversation kept returning to him, gnawing at him: her father's cruelty and destructiveness, her painful reminder that he had promised his beloved great-grandparents to protect the Heartwood, her offer of comfort and absolution for the death of Terry. He didn't want to think of these things. He began to wish he had brought Melcombe or one of the others along, not for company, but for distraction. At least he had one source of oblivion with him. He reached for the brandy bottle. Held it in his hands. Thought about how often he had turned to drink. He had lost a good friend to drink. It was a slow form of suicide, he knew. Slowly, reluctantly, he put away the brandy.

He threw himself back against the squabs, impatience joining the other seething emotions making him so uncomfortable. As he did so, his knee knocked against the portfolio. Beth's portfolio. Should he look? Was he sufficiently detached from life that he could study what he knew it contained, drawings of his childhood haunts, without being drawn into her web?

The coach lurched this way and that on wet, rutted roads. *I'll go mad, at this rate,* he thought. *Any port in a storm!* He picked up the portfolio, unwound the ribbon from around the clasp, and drew out the first of several sheaves of drawings and papers inside. They were wrapped in ribbons, both horizontally and vertically, like presents. He impatiently cast aside the ribbons from the first packet, beginning to read the top document as he did so. It was a letter from Sir James Smith, the head of the prestigious Linnean Society. It was dated in the spring.

Dear Mrs. Longford,

Thank you for sending me your excellent drawings of the flora and fauna of the woods near Whinton, Dorset, which you call the Heartwood. I am able to identify most of them, and have included their scientific names and some additional information with those items. However, several of the species are unfamiliar to me or to my colleagues. Assuming that you have drawn them accurately, they may in fact be new to the scientific world. Since your drawings of those species with which I am familiar are extremely accurate, I feel justified in entertaining this notion.

You asked that someone from the society make a visit to your woods soon, but I am afraid that is out of the question. Most of us already have commitments that will keep us busy during this summer's collecting season, alas, many of us heading for foreign shores. It is a great shame, is it not, that England's own native fauna and flora are still not completely named, while we rush to study those of the various islands and continents far across the seas?

Perhaps next year or the year after, I shall be able to come to your wood and study its creatures firsthand. You might try your local Linnean Society. As evidenced by your drawings, some of the best work on England's flora and fauna is being done by such dedicated amateurs. Unfortunately, most do not admit females as members, but someone there should be willing to look at your more unusual specimens.

It is a pity you are unwilling to collect specimens of the fauna as you have of the plant life, but such feminine qualms are quite understandable and one reason that the study of nature is and will remain in large part the province of men.

With greatest respect, I remain &c, &c.

The letter was signed with such a flourish as to be illegible.

John was impressed that such a learned man as the author of *Flora Britannica* took Beth's drawings so seriously. With a pleasurable sense of anticipation, he lifted the first drawing and held it to carriage window to take advantage of the light. It was a rendering of the Yellow Archangel, the bright yellow of its pendulous blossoms reminding him of Beth's hair. In Sir James's handwriting at the bottom, just below Beth's label, was written *Lamium galeobdolon*.

There were dozens of sketches and finished drawings, some worked up skillfully in watercolors. They were not, however, what he had expected—views of the various beloved places in and around the Heartwood, designed to wring from his heart the desire to save his heritage. Instead, they were scientific drawings of various birds, wildflowers, lizards, fish, bees, fern, even lichen. It seemed Beth had set for herself the task of depicting the living world of the Heartwood. He remembered how she had loved to sketch such things, and how he had often joined her in that pursuit. Once he had distressed her by catching and pinning butterflies, the better to depict them. He had not repeated the offense. It seemed she had grown so skilled in observation that she could draw them on the wing, with astonishing accuracy, if his own memory served him.

Memory. In spite of himself, the memories came, and he found himself lingering over this or that sketch as little incidents of childhood returned to his mind. Terry usually figured in those memories, but for the first time he found he could recall his cousin without being overwhelmed with pain and guilt. He even smiled a little, examining a perfect drawing of the little trout they used to catch in the pond near the southern end of the Heartwood. The fish were almost always too small to eat, so they were returned to the water, where they swam away with great indignation, judging from the roiling of the water about them as they fled their captors.

Before John could finish examining the first sheaf of papers, it had grown too dark to view them, so he carefully replaced them in their portfolio. He would examine them all in detail in the morning light. He smiled at his own sense of anticipation. *Not all pleasures are sensual, or at least sensual in a sexual sense,* he thought. He had known that once, but it seemed he had almost forgotten.

He was obliged to stop early for the night, as there was no moon and he didn't want his carriage to plunge over a cliff in the dark. He did not look at the portfolio when he went to his bedroom, for the week's dissipation had finally caught up with him, and he barely consumed an indifferently cooked dinner before turning in to sleep until dawn.

The next day the drenching rain had let up, to be replaced by a steady, cold drizzle. He had had enough of riding horseback under such circumstances in the peninsula. In fact, he feared the attempt would bring back unpleasant memories. So he settled himself in the traveling coach with less annoyance than usual, and took the drawings and letters out from the portfolio. In the light of day he could see that the drawings, especially the ones worked up in full color, were truly outstanding examples of the natural historian's art. No mere "lady botanizer," this! Interleaved with the drawings were letters to and from other scholars, chronicling a continuing and vain attempt by Beth to interest someone of note in natural history in coming to the woods. He felt his lips lifting in an angry snarl at the patronizing tone of many of these letters.

As he studied her drawings, he again felt some of the old magic of the Heartwood that he remembered from his childhood. Here was a drawing of the little lizard they had often seen and attempted to catch as it darted in and out of the bracken. A dragonfly that they had often admired at the pool, darting among the reeds around its perimeter, enchanted him, and the note accompanying it infuriated him. It was from a professor MacDuff of Edinburgh University, and scolded her, gently but firmly, for exaggerating the colors of the dragonfly in a note written at the bottom of Beth's drawing:

> *The Southern Hawker, which I take to be your intended subject, has almost transparent wings, and is nowhere near as colorful as you have depicted it.*

John recognized the dragonfly she represented and knew that her drawing was perfect. Was it possible that this was, indeed, a species unknown to the experts, living within the boundaries of the Heartwood?

He found one letter that was particularly poignant, from another of the naturalists she had written.

I am sorry to hear that the Heartwood is being cut down, it said.

> *If your drawings are representative, there are several species there which may not be found elsewhere in the British Isles. Would that I could come to you, but our local Linnean Society does not encourage the consideration of women's work, and I do not wish to risk my reputation upon what might be a wild goose chase. I can recommend a young man to you, but he will require a stipend of 100 pounds and a place to stay if he is to spend next summer at your Heartwood. Alas, he has told me he could not come before next summer. Can you not convince your father to stay his hand until then?*

John leafed through the drawings slowly, savoring their detail and their beauty, and, much against his will, feeling deeply the regret that he knew Beth was feeling at the destruction of the home of these plants and animals. But he was not moved to action by this regret. His detachment held. To go to Heartwood would be to face the vituperation of Beth's father, Lord Blayne.

Partly with regret, and partly with relief, John realized that there were only two drawings left. He held the first up to the window for better light, and suddenly swore and sat bolt upright. Before him on the page, in just as intricate a detail as any other drawing in the portfolio, was a portrait of a wizened old man in a coat that looked as if it might have grown from moss and lichen. He sat on a large stone, in a patch of sunlight. Portrayed in profile, he stared into the distance. He had a beak of a nose, a tangle of dark brown hair, and a crumpled hat on his head. He might have been thought just a very old man, if it had not been for the scale of the drawing.

John knew the stone. He knew the great oak tree near which it stood. That hollow in the old tree had been there when they were children, a shelter from sudden rain showers and a hiding place from which he and his cousins had planned ambushes of imagined enemies.

The size of the little old man in comparison to the stone, the tree, the hollow, made him no more than twelve to sixteen inches in height. John felt the hair on the back of his neck stand up. *She's drawn the leprechaun.* Then he corrected himself. *This is what she imagines one would look like, after hearing all of Gram's tales.*

The drawing fit so well with all of her other highly accurate and naturalistic drawings that it would have been easy to believe she had made the portrait from life, of a real creature. That there was something vaguely familiar about the little man, John was not prepared to acknowledge. With a slight tremble of his hand, he turned the next page.

He was not surprised to find another sketch of a leprechaun. But he was surprised to see that it was only that, a sketch, not a fully realized painting. It wasn't a preliminary sketch or study for the previous drawing, either. Everything about it showed less assurance on the part of the artist. In this picture, the subject faced the viewer, and was clearly feminine. And the background did not look at all like Heartwood. It looked like . . .

Suddenly he felt as if he were falling through a tunnel in time. He was six years old, and in Ireland, along with his brothers and Terry, the guests of Gram and Gramp on their Irish estate. Beth was a toddler, at home in England with her parents.

He was already skilled at evading his nurse to wander

the countryside. One spring day he managed to escape and make his way to a copse of small trees and bushes. He had been forbidden to go there, but that had only whetted his natural curiosity about everything he saw, from birds to flowers to insects. This curiosity, something he had always had in common with Beth, led him toward a beautiful and very unusual humming or buzzing sound.

He couldn't identify the bird or insect making it, and knew his best chance of seeing it was to sneak up on it. So with all the skill at his command, he crept close to the largest of the trees, which had a hollow in its base. The sound was coming from the other side of the tree. Crawling on hands and knees, stalking as carefully as ever a cat stalked its prey, he moved around the tree. He stopped, astounded, at what he saw ahead of him. A tiny little woman, no more than twelve inches tall, her face gnarled and brown as a nut, was gathering mushrooms in her apron.

He knew at once, from his great-grandmother Blayne's stories, what she was, and sprang at her without thinking, catching her unawares. Even now, twenty-one years later, he found he could remember the sturdy, strong little body twisting in his. He had called out to her not to be afraid, he didn't want to hurt her, or take her gold, or anything like that, he only wanted to speak with her for a moment.

But the terrified creature had bit him, hard, on the arm, and he had dropped her. She clambered between his legs and made straight toward the hollow in the tree, disappearing into its darkness. Shock at the painful bite temporarily rooted him in place. But curiosity drove him on in spite of the blood flowing down his arm. When he reached the tree, he found that the hollowed-out portion of the trunk was neither deep nor wide. It would have admitted the little woman, but it couldn't have hidden her. Examine it as he would, he could find no sign of a door or any other sort of opening. After digging in the damp leaf litter at the bottom of the hollow and examining every inch of it from top to bottom and side to side, he sat down and pondered the situation. Were it not for the small but unmistakable imprint of sharp teeth on his arm, with blood oozing from the deepest part of the bite, he would have thought he had imagined the whole episode.

He had hurried home and told Terry, who had been both skeptical and fascinated. But having run away from his nurse and gone to a place he had been expressly forbidden to explore, John feared to tell the tale to his great-grandparents. The two boys had kept it a secret between them.

Long before he had grown to manhood, the whole episode had faded until he thought it was an imagined event, not a memory.

When Beth had seen a leprechaun, or thought she had, he had not laughed at her. It had been a bond between them, though he did not know whether to believe either of them had actually seen the legendary creatures. His great-grandmother, his beloved Gram, had not believed he had seen a female, so why should he?

Beth had never doubted, though. She had considered him a member of the band of leprechaun believers, along with their great-grandmother, and possibly, though they could never be sure, their great-grandfather. Through the years, though his own memory faded to nothingness, he had indulged her belief, as he had indulged their beloved Gram, out of kindness. He had thought Beth would outgrow it all, as he had.

On her visit to the abbey Beth had tried to remind him they had each seen leprechauns, and he had savagely rejected the notion. But this picture drew him back to that time and place and made it seem very, very real. How could Beth, who, to his knowledge, had never been to Ireland, have been able to depict that very place he had once thought he held a leprechaun? It was drawn tentatively, not with the sure, realistic touch of her other drawings. It was almost as if someone had described the setting to her, and the lady leprechaun too. But he knew he had never done so.

He turned back to the picture of the male leprechaun on the stone. It was drawn with the same precision and attention to detail as her pictures of birds, flowers, insects, and lizards. Something told him, something he could not deny even though he wanted to, that it had been drawn from life. And the sketch of the female? If he had not described the creature to her in detail, had not described the place where he had seen it, how had she managed to sketch it sufficiently to make it recognizable?

Because Shamus told her, came the thought. Unbidden, unwanted, annoying, but unshakable, the conviction grew in him that his leprechaun and the place John had seen her had been described by Beth's leprechaun, while sitting with her in the Heartwood.

Chapter 7

John banged sharply on the roof of the carriage. Whiting opened the little door to ask if something was wrong.

"Very wrong," he replied. "Turn this carriage around as soon as possible. We are turning back."

"Back, my lord?"

"Yes, back. First to Wayneathe, and then we go to Dorset. I find I have important business at Blayne Manor."

Whiting made no response. John could just imagine his serious face working as he tried to figure out this latest start of his employer, whom he had know since he was a boy in short pants. *I hope he may figure it out,* John thought. *I can't!*

When they reached Wayneathe Abbey, repairs on the priory were already underway. Nothing could have exceeded Basporth's astonishment at finding his employer at the door. He frowned in puzzlement. "My lord?"

"I am going to Blayne Manor for a visit. As my valet is in Scotland, you must pack for me, I fear. I will need a wardrobe suitable for a visit to a country estate. Including evening wear, I suppose."

"Of course, my lord." Questions he dared not ask contorted the elderly retainer's face.

John took pity on him. "I have decided I gave my cousin short shrift. I have fences to mend, with her, and if possible with her father."

THE LAST LEPRECHAUN

"Shall I send for your valet to join you there?"

John frowned. His current valet suited the kind of master he served: willing, nay, eager to procure lovely women for his master's bed, he was no less assiduous in finding willing maids to grace his own. He was a sly man, with considerably less culture or moral turpitude than John would have accepted before his slump into decadence.

"No. Let him stay in Scotland, in case any of my erstwhile friends show up. He can show them the door for me, and when I have finished my business in Dorset it may be I will still have time for a little shooting. I doubt I shall be long, a fortnight at the most."

Basporth arranged his face into a mask of indifference once more, but John was not deceived. His butler was pleased by his decision to go to Blayne manor.

Fortunately for John's sanity, the weather made it possible for him to ride ahead of the carriage most of the way from Cornwall to Dorset. When he reached the top of the downs and looked out over the broad sweep of Blackmore Vale, he felt an odd pang of joy and longing as his eyes searched for Whintonvale, the little wooded valley within the larger vale, which held the Blayne woodlands and the tiny village of Whinton. He eagerly rode up the hill that looked out over Blayne Manor, its park and grounds, just as the sun began to set. It should have been a stirring sight, for the view was magnificent, with woods on one side and the folds of hills falling away in the distance behind the stone manor, a rambling yet harmonious combination of building styles over the centuries. John turned his head instinctively to look at the woods, both managed and protected, which began just beyond the meadow to the east of the Blayne estate, richly green and inviting in the summer, pleasantly gloomy in the winter. Just now the trees on the exposed heights would be putting on their fall colors, while down in the protected lower ground, summer would still reign.

He drew in a sharp breath as his eyes took in what he could see in the deepening dusk. At the boundary of the park meadows, trees had once stood shoulder to shoulder, beech and walnut and lime, with the occasional oak towering over. As this part of the woods near the manor was managed for fuel, shingles, bark for the tanner, and barrel staves, he was prepared to see occasional gaps where trees had recently been pollarded or coppiced, but now a wasteland of stumps and felled trees met his eyes. He was unprepared for the shaft of pain that shot through him as this denudation—no, this desecration—of the woodlands.

Mouth set in a grim line, he urged his horse down the lane that led to Blayne Manor, the light of battle in his eye.

The servant who opened the door was not one John remembered from his childhood, and seemed not to recognize his name, though he was properly impressed by his title. Perhaps this lack of recognition explained why John was led upstairs to his uncle's smoking room. This masculine sanctum had been created by his great-grandfather because his beloved wife became ill when exposed to tobacco in any form, so her husband had added on a solid room, well ventilated to the outside, in which to enjoy his cigars and pipes.

John doubted any such consideration accounted for the current Lord Blayne's continued preference for the smoking room. He cared little for the opinion of his wife. Rather, it had become by this time a hallowed place of masculine retreat, where the lord of the manor could spend much of his time smoking, drinking, and even, in the case of Beth's father, whoring, when a servant girl could be snagged.

Sure enough, tobacco fumes engulfed John when he entered the room, and several hounds briefly glanced his way before going back to their slumber before the fire. When Lord Blayne heard him announced, he sprang from his chair with an oath.

"What the devil are you doing here?"

From his unsteady posture and thickened pronunciation, John knew the baron was at that stage when he had begun to feel the effects of drink but was not yet incapable of either logical thought or action.

"I've come for a short visit, uncle."

"Long overdue, not that I want you."

"No, you've made that clear enough, but I thought face to face . . ."

"Face to face, I can tell you how much I despise you." Lord Blayne sneered. "But you know that. It's the woods, isn't it? Beth went to see you, to tell you about the woods. Well, it will do you no good. The cutting goes on, and damn the entail. I've thirty men cutting. By the time you have gone through the courts about it, there won't be a tree between here and the river Stour."

John shook his head. "In truth, it wasn't about the woods that I came, but I am curious. Why, uncle? Why cut down the woods? Is it just for the money? Is it spite? You're not hurting me. I don't care one way or another."

"No, you don't give a damn about anything having to do with the Blayne barony, damn your hide. Get out!"

"It's true enough that I don't care to tell you how to run your own property. The only one you are hurting is Beth, your daughter, who loves those woods and always has."

"Hah!" A fanatical light came into Blayne's eyes. "Not the only one who loves them. I'll have him out of there. Out, I say. Bad luck, thrice over. Wicked, vicious beast. I'll destroy his cosy little nest. Once every tree in the Heartwood is down he'll have nowhere to hide. If necessary, I'll grub out every stump, dig up every burrow, excavate up every tunnel. I'll dig ten feet deep from here to the Stour."

Lord Blayne's face had become increasingly purple during this speech. Spittle collected at the corner of his mouth, and a wild look flashed in his eyes.

"To whom are you referring, Uncle?"

Blayne's mouth worked soundlessly for a moment. "You know!" He shook a finger at John. "She said you knew."

John shook his head. "Tell me."

A look no less mad, but more calculating, shifted over Blayne's features. "Why, a thief, that's who. A pernicious thief who's been plaguing the neighborhood."

"Quite a lot of effort to go after one thief, uncle. What has he stolen to make it worth your while?"

"Must be a pack of them. Using the woods as their hiding place. Things disappearing everywhere. Honest citizens not safe. But we'll have 'em out!" At this, Blayne sank into his chair, exhausted. "Have 'em out." He reached for a brandy bottle and drank directly from it.

John took the chair opposite his in front of the fire. "I'll be surprised if you are able to get your men to cut down the Heartwood. The plantations and managed woods, yes. But the Heartwood? Folks around here have always had a sort of superstitious dread about that area—one reason it has been possible to preserve it for so long from encroachment by wood gleaners and poachers."

"For enough gold, some men will do anything. But you're right. The fools need the work, but I had to bring in more than half my workers from outside the county. Housing them all about the estate. Bunch of rum 'uns, too. Be glad when it's done with."

"How long do you think it will take, then, uncle?"

Blayne lifted his head from contemplation of the fire. "Six weeks. I've offered a bonus for doing it sooner, but some of those trees are huge."

"Some of those trees have been growing since before the conquest. It seems a shame . . ."

"Spare me your tears. Should have been cut long ago like the rest of England's trees, or managed properly—coppiced or pollarded. I'll turn 'em into cultivated fields.

More income this way. Those woods are a dead drain on the estate. I'm doing you a favor."

"I told you I don't care about the money, one way or the other." John stood. "I'll pay my respects to Lady Blayne and Beth if they are still up."

"Hah! Pay 'em if you like. Won't do you any good. You can't have her."

"I beg your pardon, sir?"

"Beth. Can't have her. Knew you'd want her if you saw her. Every man does. But you—never. I'll never consent."

John sat back down again. He had no intention of marrying Beth or anyone else, but he found something in him rebelled against being told he couldn't do so.

"May I ask why?"

"Have my daughter marry my son's murderer! Ghoulish! Just as your being here is. Go away. You are not wanted here!"

John winced. Beth had said he wasn't responsible. He knew he wasn't responsible, on a rational level. But still, somehow, the guilt would not let go of him.

"I have written to you of my deep regret . . ."

"Will your regret bring Terry back?"

John put his head in his hands and shook it wearily. "Nothing will. For either of us. So why continue this enmity?"

"Why? The Blayne barony will be subsumed in your title, though it is centuries older. Unnatural business, that, your branch of the family receiving a title above the ancestral one. Busy, ambitious men, your grandfather and father. Gramp was proud of them, damn his eyes! Yet their climb to power and wealth means that our title, the Blayne name, will die out. It is older, it is honorable, it . . ."

John looked up. "I had no idea you cared so much about the family name, and especially its honor."

Blayne blanched and jumped up, making John do

likewise. The two men stood confronting one another, almost nose to nose.

"You've no notion of my feelings. D'you think, just because I've lived my life for pleasure, as I hear you are doing now, I have no sense of my place in society? No sense of my family? Well, you're wrong. I do. And I am going to resurrect the Blayne barony, as an independent title, through my daughter."

John's look of surprise had the older man chuckling. "Thrown you a facer, hasn't it! I will find a candidate for her hand. Eligible, wealthy, but not titled. If she'll marry him and bears him a son, I'll be able to petition to have the barony pass through the female line. No wonder you have come sniffing after her. Want to put a spoke in my wheels, don't you? But you shan't have Beth! I couldn't bear it. You are responsible for Terry's death. To let you have Beth would be to reward you. The barony, the estates, my daughter. Haven't you caused me enough grief? Get out!"

And to John's horror, the older man suddenly began to weep. He wanted to stay, to protest his innocence, though he had not conquered his own feelings of guilt. But he was so embarrassed and distressed by his uncle's open weeping that he did what he had never done in battle—he fled.

John found Lady Blayne in her own sitting room upstairs, stretched out on a sofa. She had always been fragile, but as he beheld her he saw a woman who had faded almost to a wraith.

"John!" She called out to him in delight, and held out her hand, though she did not rise from her sofa. He knelt to kiss her hand, and then, when she drew him closer, hugged her gently. He felt little but bones, and embraced her as gently as possible. When he sat back on his heels, he saw tears in her eyes, and felt answering ones in his own.

"You are not well," he said.

She chuckled. "When have you ever known me to be well, John? But I am much better for seeing you. Pull up a chair, and tell me that Beth's account of you is greatly exaggerated."

John felt a flush mount his cheeks. "I hope she has not told you too much of what is, I fear, a sad truth. I am a dissipated, wicked man, aunt."

"Nonsense. Dissipated, I can see well enough." She traced the furrows around his eyes and mouth. "Wicked? Never!"

At least his aunt did not blame him for her son's death. Holding her hands gently in his, he talked with her for a while about the old days. She seemed to derive great pleasure from remembering episodes from the past when all the children—hers and their cousins'—were running wild over Blayne Manor and its nearby fields and woods. At last he got up, feeling that she was tiring. "I had best go. You need your rest, and I expect I will need to find lodgings in Whinton, as your husband dislikes me so. Is Beth still up? I would like to speak with her before I go."

"Beth is not here. After checking on me, she went to Hintock cottage, on the far side of the woods, to spend a few days. It is hers now, you know, along with their land."

John was surprised to hear that Beth was in possession of Hintock cottage, formerly the property of an eccentric old couple who had viewed the Blaynes with hostility—primarily because they did not manage the Heartwood as they should, but let it run riot, which offended the Hintock's views of proper management.

"She owns the Hintock property now?"

Lady Blayne nodded. "Sometimes I stay there with her. But Blayne does not like it, and always forces me to return here eventually. She used to come here almost every day, to see to me and to attend to estate matters, but it upsets her so to see the trees disappearing day by day that she can hardly bear to do so anymore."

Tears stood in Lady Blayne's eyes. "All this hate and confrontation over a mythical creature. I sometimes wonder if both my husband and my daughter are slightly insane."

"Then it *is* about the leprechaun?"

"So-called. I begin to think this belief is a sort of madness in the Blayne blood."

Perhaps it is, John thought, remembering what had brought him here. "I can understand why Beth seeks to save the woods, and the leprechaun, if such there be. After all, our great-grandparents bequeathed to her their love of the woods, and belief in the leprechaun they both credited with their coming together as man and wife. But how did your husband come to believe in the leprechaun, and why does he hate him so?"

"I don't know. It's a mystery to me. He never tells me anything. But somehow he blames the creature for all his recent misfortunes, from his gambling losses to Terry's death. He's been determined to murder this nonexistent creature ever since he learned of our son's—" Abruptly Lady Blayne's face crumpled and she wept.

"Oh, Aunt Lillian. I don't know what to say. I feel so terrible . . ."

"No, John, you shouldn't." She sobbed the words out, grasping at the handkerchief he offered her. "I don't blame you. Foolish of Blayne to do so. Terrence was a casualty of a terrible battle. That's all, and how Blayne can blame you for it, I don't know."

John knew. "He entered the army when Napoleon escaped, but he had always wanted to be a soldier like me. Your husband feels that is why he joined. And then, on the day he died, I was standing right beside him. I was probably the sniper's target, because I was carrying dispatches from Wellington. That's why."

"Still not your fault," his aunt gulped. "I know it. Beth knows it. If Terry were here, he'd say so. Don't you dare look so! Beth told me you blamed yourself. Don't you dare!"

THE LAST LEPRECHAUN

John was startled by the vehemence with which this usually meek woman asserted these words. They were as a balm to a deep, festering wound.

"You're the bravest, finest young man I know, and you served your country heroically." She held out her hands to him, and when he took them, squeezed hard, as hard as her slight strength would allow. "Give that foolish notion up, for my sake. You can't help with Blayne if you keep it, for he will use it against you. And we desperately need help with him, my dear."

John inwardly shrank from her words. He had come here for selfish reasons, to discover the truth of the leprechaun's existence, to see it for himself if he could. Curiosity, a pleasure he had almost forgotten, had driven him here. He hadn't any intention of involving himself in the Blaynes's problems, nor anyone else's. He was going to spend the rest of his life, however short or long it might be, in the pursuit of sensual pleasure. Wasn't he? But he found himself holding his fragile aunt in his arms, comforting her as she comforted him, and something in him that he thought had died stirred to life again.

Chapter 8

John awoke early the next morning, feeling better rested than he had in years. Lady Blayne had insisted he stay the night, assuring him her husband would drink himself into a stupor and then stay in bed until noon.

"He'll never know you've been here, dear, and if he does, why, what is that? You are his heir, after all."

So he had allowed this motherly woman to treat him as she always had, as a son. It had given her pleasure, clearly, to mother him a bit, and did him no harm. *Perhaps even some good.* John thrust back the memory of his own mother, who had loved him, but who had traveled so much with his father that she had been unable to spend much time with her children.

Dawn's light falling on his face awoke him, and he hastily dressed in the riding clothes he had worn the day before and made his way to the kitchen. There he found a few servants who remembered him from the old days, and he had some difficulty escaping their joyful attentions. He walked out the kitchen door with a well-laden picnic basket swinging from his right hand, and Beth's portfolio tucked under his left arm.

His goal was the Hintock cottage, which Beth had somehow acquired, and which lay at the eastern edge of the Heartwood on the other side of St. Anne's Water. He knew the cottage well. The Hintocks had been independent farmers who cherished their small estate and treated it as their fiefdom, defending it from all encroachment by the Blaynes, their children, guests, and hunters of all sorts. On their side of the Heartwood's stone fence they had managed their woods as was customary, with some trees coppiced and some pollarded every few years, to provide a continuing supply of wood for fuel, shingles, and basketry materials. It had been a profitable operation for them, and they made their contempt of the Blaynes known, asking, "Why waste a perfectly good woods, just letting it sit there, growing and dying, without so much as picking up windfalls?"

This outwardly truculent and reclusive couple had actually been quite welcoming to the children who dared to breach their defenses. Young Blaynes had eaten sweet biscuits made by this goodwife's hands. When they brought her berries, she would bake them into the best pies, as the cousins declared, to be found in all of England.

Though sad to learn that the Hintocks had passed on, John was glad to know the lovely old cottage and its acres were in Beth's hands. He felt relief that she had a place of refuge from her drunken father, who was trying to get her to remarry for his benefit, not hers. What right had her father, after all, to say whom she could or could not marry? She was of age, and a widow too. She was not under her father's control. Who was this suitor Blayne had in mind for her?

When his thoughts turned in this direction, John hastily diverted them into a survey of his surroundings. Once he had passed the kitchen gardens and the stable block, he reached what had been the meadow that lay between the manor and the woods. It wasn't a meadow any longer, but a chewed up, tool-strewn encampment where workmen sharpened axes and saws and ate breakfasts cooked over wood fires. And beyond the meadow?

There was no beyond the meadow, not for a long way.

Where once old trees had soared skyward, the sky came down to meet stumps and logs. Once again, even stronger, he felt that chill, that stab of pain that had shafted through him the night before when first he had glimpsed the carnage. It looked a little like battle, he thought, and suddenly the broken trees became broken bodies of horses and men, and the morning mist the smoke of cannon and musket. Nausea overcame him and he closed his eyes, swaying on his feet as unwelcome memories transformed themselves into sights and smells and sounds.

"Be ye Lord John?" a deep voice asked him.

He turned around, staring blankly at the workmen preparing for their day. He saw before him a burly man of perhaps fifty.

"I am." He held out his hand to the man, at last recognizing in him the groom who had always seen after his horses when he visited Blayne manor. "Jacob Smith, isn't it?"

"Ah, to think you remember me! What a fine gentleman ye've become, my lord. I guess 'tisn't Lord John now, but Lord Wayneathe?" Jacob hesitated at the proffered hand, but then, when John continued holding his out, took it in a crushing grip.

A few minutes' questioning brought Jacob's history to light. After his grandfather's death, the new Lord Blayne had gambled away so much of his assets that he could no longer afford to keep up the once-famous stables. Jacob had lost his job, leaving him with little means to support his family, then numbering four "still at home" and an ailing wife.

"It be a doleful work, my lord," Jacob said. "A doleful work, and one we'll regret in these parts, mind. Particular the cutting of the trees in the Heartwood and around St. Anne's Well. But I must have food for my family."

"I understand," John said. Then Jacob's words sank in. "The well? You mean where the villagers hold May Day festivities each year?" He pictured in his mind the well, set in a little clearing just inside the Heartwood, nearer the vicar's cottage in Whinton than to Blayne manor, and within walking distance of the village's main street. The spring was of ancient origin, capped by a stone-sided bowl covered by an iron grate, from which flowed a generous stream of clear, pure water. Known as St. Anne's Water, it was this stream that gurgled through the wood, down the ravine and into the pool near the southern end of the Heartwood. Overflowing from there, its waters eventually mingled with the River Stour. One of the three gates into the Heartwood permitted villagers to enter just opposite the vicar's cottage on special days to visit the well and picnic or dance in the small meadow. It was kept locked, but by custom the key was made available to the village's vicar for such occasions.

"That I do, my lord. *St. Anne's* Well!" To John's surprise, Jacob's tone was sarcastic. He spat to one side. According to official church history, a Christian saint had been martyred there attempting to save a red deer with a white cross on its side from heathen hunters. Water sprang up where she fell, and with her dying breath she had requested that the land through which the spring flowed be set aside for wild creatures, untouched by the hand of man. This was the story enshrined in Christian history. But the spring had flowed there, so the local stories went, long before any Christian set foot in England, and was protected, in truth, by far older than Christian spirits.

"Lord Blayne means to put a stone over it and shut it down. Ancient folks they was, what built it, and ancient the curse for disturbing it," Jacob said in a portentous tone. "I told Lord Blayne I'd cut his outer woods, but not one finger would I put to that place. He says as how the men he's brought in will do it, and they might. A puny lot they be, but the ones from Lunnon are not afeard of the old 'uns, or the little people either."

"But why would he want to tear that down? Those few trees can hardly be worth depriving the village of such a lovely spot? And why shut up the stream?"

"I dunno, my lord." Jacob's expression told John that he held much the same opinion of Lord Blayne's state of mind as John did, but of course he dared not say so.

"What wages does he pay you?"

"Fifteen shillings a week, m'lord, and a bonus if we finish by All Hallow's Eve."

Rich wages indeed for this kind of work. No wonder my uncle is able to recruit desperate men, even those who fear the consequences for their future.

John nodded. "Well, I expect I'd best let you get to it." And he turned back around, heading for the closest area where the wood remained untouched, not allowing himself any more glances around at the fallen trees which had triggered that sudden, nasty memory. As he neared the wood, he had to stop and watch, for his own safety's sake, the completion of the cutting down of a large tree. It seemed to shriek as its weight tore through the remaining trunk and it fell to the ground, which shook from the impact. A loud, triumphant shout came from the men who had felled it, and they immediately began the task of dismembering it, hacking and sawing at limbs as large as good-sized trees themselves. Ox teams stood by to drag away the wood.

John walked on, climbing over limbs and shuffling through branches, his boots much the worse for the experience. At last he passed through what survived of the managed woods. He estimated about one-third of those trees had already been cut. Ahead lay the tall stone wall which surrounded the protected woods. He hurried to the Heartwood's western gate, which he opened with the key he brought from Blayne Manor. Once inside, it took him a while to walk far enough into the wood, following a narrow trail, to escape the sounds of the logging operation and once again feel the enchantment of the place as he had as a child.

The silence of the wood had always struck him, though it was not truly silent. Bird calls, the whirr of insect wings, the rustle of leaves, the chatter of squirrels, all could be heard by the attentive ear. Yet these sounds were so different from man-made sounds, and so soothing, that they seemed like a restful, almost magical silence. He found himself treading lightly, to avoid disturbing . . . what? The forest itself?

Preoccupied with memories, he had walked quite a ways before realizing that the little path he trod was the very one along which he and Terry had passed when they had found Beth so long ago. Moving as quietly as he could, he slowly looked all around him, not wishing even to admit to himself what he hoped to see. Stealthily he proceeded to the edge of the ravine, that ancient earthslip which provided St. Anne's Water with its path to the Stour. He felt deeply once again the horror he had known when thinking little Beth might have fallen into that deep chasm. *Another terrible memory,* he thought, yet it was quickly followed by a joyful one: the sound of Beth's happy laughter from her perch on a rock by the side of the ravine.

When he found the rock, perhaps in fact an ancient standing stone, long since fallen, on which Beth had sat that day, he looked about him more carefully than he ever had before. Sure enough, not far away he found a tree with a large hollow space at the base of the trunk. He knelt, pushing aside the undergrowth, and looked inside. He could not see all of the interior, so he felt, gently but thoroughly, all around the hollow core of the old tree. He found nothing to indicate that it gave access to a hidden space, either behind or beneath the hollow. He sat up with a sigh and looked around him.

Who is the madman, or woman, he wondered, contemplating the way he had ridiculed Beth and passed harsh judgement on Lord Blayne. *The Earl of Wayneathe, looking for a leprechaun! A good thing no one knows.* But foolish as he felt now, that was exactly why he had come back to the Heartwood.

Suddenly he felt a prickle on the back of his neck, as if he were being observed. That warning prickle had saved his life several times in battle. But long, careful study of the trees overhead and the ground around him revealed nothing the least bit menacing. No whisper of stealthy approach suggested an enemy. Neither did a small, gnarled face peer at him from the trees or shrubs. Yet the birds had grown oddly silent, and even the buzzing of insects seemed temporarily to have ceased. He had the odd fancy that the forest was holding its breath, and realized that he was holding his. He blew it out in an exasperated snort and stood.

Chapter 9

John returned to the rock and looked over the precipice, where the woods abruptly ended in a rocky cliff. Little Beth had sat on that rock, inches from this drop-off, chatting, she had said, with a leprechaun. A few steps further and she might well have taken a fatal tumble. He looked back over his shoulder at the ancient tree near the rock, and said out loud, "Thank you." There was no reply; surely he hadn't expected one, and yet he felt no embarrassment for having spoken.

He began to move downhill along the cliff face, wending his way among the shrubs and ancient tree roots that erosion had exposed. The cliff began to disintegrate, he knew, as the land sloped toward the south. Soon steep walls became boulders, which gave way to giant rocks, and then to a series of stepping stones, down to a small forest pool. Known by the villagers as Dead Boy's Sink, it was a beautiful spot which traced its ugly name back to a long ago series of drownings. He and his cousins had referred to it simply as "the pool." In the distance he could hear the murmur of water as it flowed over the natural rock dam that made the pool. He made his way down carefully, aware that he was no longer the agile boy who had bounded from rock to rock on his way down to the bank of the pristine clear pool where once he and Terry had tickled trout while stretched out on rocky ledges, or dared one another to plunge in for a brief, icy swim on warm summer days. These were forbidden pleasures, for their great-grandparents had always warned them not to swim there.

When John reached his goal, he found the idyllic pool of his youth replaced by a disgusting swamp of murky, mud-filled water. Along its edges, dead fish and frogs sloshed gently against the rocks. A raven flew up from one of their decaying bodies with a startled cry.

He looked upstream, and saw that the water ran dark instead of clear. He realized the cutting of the woods upstream had allowed the soil to wash down St. Anne's Water to this, one of the loveliest parts of the Heartwood, destroying it. Anger bubbled in him. He hastened downstream, past the waterfall, to the third Heartwood gate, which opened next to a small low-water footbridge across St. Anne's Water. John used his key to open the gate. On the other side of the footbridge, the less elaborate wooden gate the Hintocks had put up to prevent encroachment on their land had fallen into disrepair. It had never presented much of a challenge to active children, and today he had merely to stride over it, intending to hasten to Hintock cottage. But before he had gone three strides, he was startled to see Beth sitting on a fallen log some yards back from the overgrown path. She had been sitting so still, and was so well camouflaged in a brown cloak with the hood up, covering her bright hair, that he had almost passed by her.

She'd been watching his approach, and when their eyes met, she showed no evidence of joy. Rather, she looked wary, like some woodland creature trying to decide whether to flee. Her eyes turned to the portfolio under his arm.

"You came."

"I had to return your property to you, didn't I?"

"You looked through it, then." Beth knew that if he had not, he would have sent it by a servant or through the mail.

John dropped down beside her on the log. "Yes. You've become a remarkable artist, Beth."

"An illustrator," she corrected him. "Of natural history. I've become an expert on the flora and fauna of Heartwood." There was pride in her voice.

"Yes. Your drawings are remarkably accurate."

"Were I not a woman, I would be an influential member of the Dorset Botanical Society." Slight bitterness turned down her mouth. "Everything in them was drawn from life. Well, everything but the last."

John didn't want to deal with that yet. "The trout in the pool . . ." His voice broke, and he cleared his throat.

"Professor MacDuff said the markings on them indicated a subspecies perhaps known only to that pool."

"They are all gone now, I suppose? The ravens are eating well there."

"I suppose so. When all their prey disappears, the ravens too will go, along with everything else." She turned her head away and struggled for control, while John fought to keep from putting his arms around her to comfort her. At last she turned back, her lower lip scarlet where she had bitten it to keep from crying.

"Have you come back to help, or to see me locked up as a madwoman?"

"It is your father who is mad, it seems."

"Why, because he admits to seeing the leprechaun?"

"No. He never admitted it, though it was clear that he has. It is his hatred of the creature that is driving the destruction."

"Then you believe . . ."

He opened the portfolio and turned to the next-to-last drawing. "You said this was drawn from the life?"

"Yes."

"And not from childhood memories, I'm guessing."

"No."

She looked steadily at him, and he at her, for a long time.

"How did that work? Did he actually sit for you?" He felt the sane, skeptical part of himself bubbling up in laughter at the thought of a leprechaun, a mythical being, sitting calmly for its portrait.

"In fact, he did. I'd been sketching him from memory for years, from the brief glimpses I'd get of him. When Father started cutting the woods, Shamus agreed to let me draw him. He'd only sit for a few minutes at a time, and each time in a different place, to avoid capture. He is very afraid, and with good reason. But he is the last of his kind, and wanted there to be a record. Not that anyone will believe it, I suppose, but you and me. And Father, though he'll deny it. He's sane enough not to wish to be locked up for believing in leprechauns. More likely to have me put away, if he can. He'd get the rest of the woods, the few acres I own, and cut them down, too. I hope you didn't show him this."

John shook his head.

"How did your interview with him go?"

"He would have thrown me out, but he was too drunk."

Beth smiled bitterly. "Yes, the drink will kill him. But not in time, unfortunately. I see you think me hard."

"I know you have reason not to love your father."

"Even more than you can suppose."

John gently traced the outline of the drawing with his fingers. "Portrait of a leprechaun. The last of his kind." He lingered over the picture, studying it carefully. "Drawn from life." He then slowly turned the page to the sketch of the female.

"But not this one."

"No, she was described to me."

"I never described her in such detail. Indeed, I don't remember describing her to you at all."

"Not you. Him. Shamus. I told him about your having seen her once. He didn't believe me. He thought her long dead by then. Still, he told me how she looked. I remembered you said she was gathering mushrooms, so he described the area for me. He'd get very frustrated with my efforts, but it is difficult to draw something someone else describes to you. He said it was a fair likeness."

"It is. Not quite exact, but close. The spinney is just as I remembered it, and the tree, but there is something lacking in the female's portrait. I saw her so briefly, it is difficult to put my finger on just what."

Suddenly Beth began to cry silently. Her eyes reddened, great tears rolled down her cheeks and she let them flow unchecked as she looked at him.

"Why, what is it? I meant no insult."

"You believe me! You believe in them! Oh, John." She leaned forward, took the lapels of his coat in her hands, and gave him a little shake. "You can't imagine what it means to me. I thought you'd call me mad. I often wondered if I could be mad."

"If I hadn't seen her myself, I might." He could no longer resist putting his arms around her. He drew her close, and she rested her head against his chest, little sobs and shudders shaking her body for a while. When she pulled away, fumbling in her sleeve for a handkerchief, he offered her his.

"You denied having seen her."

"I didn't remember until I saw this drawing. That brought it all back."

"You'll help, then?"

Whether it was because his devotion to pleasure had waned, or because he had derived more pleasure from holding her than he was ready to recognize, John did not know. But he felt himself nodding his head. "But how? I cannot declare your father mad for believing something to be true. Why does he hate the little fellow so?"

Beth stood. "It is a long story. I've much to tell you. Will you come to Hintock cottage for tea?"

He agreed, and followed her down the path, much better worn on her side of the fence than the Blayne side. He allowed himself to enjoy the twitch of her posterior beneath her supple woolen cloak, and as soon as they could walk abreast, he took her hand and kissed it. She stopped and looked up into his face. Anger suddenly washed through her; he could see her color redden, not from embarrassment, and saw that she withdrew much more than just her hand from his. He could scarcely maintain eye contact, so disgusted was the look she gave him.

"I don't want your help for any reason but the right one."

He smiled, trying for the rakish look which had charmed a hundred females of every class. "And what might be the right one?"

"It certainly doesn't involve love-making! You must help me because it is the right thing to do. For that reason and that only. Otherwise, turn back to Blayne Manor now. You'll find much more in common with my father than with me." She hastened away, leaving him stunned and angry. How dare she again compare him with that drunken sot?

Because you are becoming like him, said that voice in his head that occasionally disturbed his rounds of revelry. Beth's father always tumbled every female he could get his hands on, drank too much, hunted and gamed to excess, and considered "duty" an obscene word. He remembered his father shaking his head over Lord Blayne's excesses and saying he hoped his cousin would die before he had only a ruined shell of an inheritance to pass on to Terry.

Terry, too, had ignored duty, in a way, by going off to fight at Waterloo even though he was his father's only son. He had gone, an eager, fiery, inexperienced soldier, into the maelstrom of Waterloo, acquitted himself bravely, and then died while pausing a moment to talk with his cousin. If they had both put duty first that day?

John shuddered, remembering in spite of himself. He

had stopped and dismounted to talk briefly with Terry before continuing on his way to carry a dispatch back to Wellington, when the shot had rung out from a tree nearby. An enemy sniper had fired at him just as he started to put his foot in the stirrup, and the bullet meant for him had bloomed, an obscene flower, in Terry's abdomen.

John was almost overpowered by the memory. He had the urge to race back up the path the Blayne Manor, to get on his horse and flee to his Scottish hunting box. There he would be distracted by days of mindless tramping over hills and dales and nights of flowing wine and raucous jokes with whomever he could get to join him.

Beth had disappeared from view by the time he had mastered himself. *I'm not Blayne, and don't want to become him,* he thought. *Besides, not all pleasure is sensual. I find the challenge of tracking down and perhaps saving the last leprechaun quite enticing.*

Beth had a kettle on the stove and a plate of bread and butter, a little shaved ham, and some sweet biscuits arranged on a platter when he arrived. He had gone in stinctively to the back door, where he and the other children had always come when Mrs. Hintock had been alive and so oddly delighted to welcome the little visitors she and her husband always pretended they wanted to keep away. He opened it and walked in. Beth was in the act of lifting the heavy kettle from the stove. He took it from her and carried it to the kitchen table. She lifted the lid from the teapot, and he poured until she said stop, then replaced the kettle on the stove.

"It all looks so much the same. I can almost imagine Mrs. Hintock walking in any second."

Beth smiled, though her eyes were wary. "She was an old dear. Did you know she left the place to me?"

"No, I thought perhaps Longford had purchased it for you with your dowry."

Beth snorted. "Certainly not. I went to Longford

without a penny. I nursed Mr. Hintock when he was ill, and visited her often. Parish duties by the vicar's wife, you might say, but she was special to me, and I to her. After Longford died, my father threw me out for not remarrying to please him, so I came to her here. Still, I never expected this. She had no children, no close relatives, and it seems that she and her husband had made the same provision in case she should die first and then he. They knew how I loved the wood, the meadows. I made many of my drawings right here on this kitchen table."

Beth was not ordinarily a watering pot, but she felt the tears welling up again, so she turned away, busying herself with the tea.

"Where's your dragon?"

"Mavis?" Beth smiled at his apt description of her maid. "She walked over to Whinton to visit her sister. She'll doubtless have a fit if she discovers that we were here alone. But I am safe. I meant what I said, John. You mustn't do it because you wish to be my lover . . ." She saw him start to protest and held up her hand. "Or even my husband. I won't remarry, so that leaves no room for anything but friendship between us."

John wondered at the adamant tone with which she said she wouldn't remarry, but since he had no intention of marrying her, he let it pass. "If I can help, I will, for two reasons."

"What are they?" She stood still as a doe about to decide to flee.

"First of all, to satisfy my curiosity. I want to see this creature, to talk with him. That is what brought me here."

She nodded. "You always were the curious sort. What is the other?"

"Just the reason you suggested—because it is the right thing to do. It seems to me the best thing would be to help the little fellow get back to Ireland."

"He won't go. He was banished from faery, and says he has no more chance of surviving aboveground in Ireland than here. It would only prolong his lonely existence, he says. He is resigned to his fate."

"Why does he say he is the last of his kind, when I saw a female, alive and very healthy, only a few years before you encountered him?"

"He doesn't believe you. She was torn apart by dogs. Dogs are their great enemies, especially once the trees are cut down so they have no sanctuary."

"Yes, I remember the story of her death, and that it happened many years before any of us were born. Our great-grandparents were only recently wed at the time. I tried to tell Gram what I'd seen, but she didn't believe me."

Suddenly John knew what was missing from the picture Beth had drawn of his lady leprechaun.

"Where is your portfolio? Get it for me. Quickly."

Puzzled, Beth did as he requested, leaving the room briefly and returning with it. He pulled out the sheaf of drawings and turned to the last one. "Get your pencils. You need to add something. Here," he said, pointing to a place on her cheek. "And here. And here. And on her hands, too."

"What, John?"

"Scars. White against the brown of her skin. It's been a long time, but I can see them just as clearly as then. I thought at the time they were a tatoo or natural pattern of some sort, but now I think they must have been scars."

"He . . . he never mentioned scars or tattoos. This could mean . . . oh, John, do you think it possible?"

"That Shamus is not the last leprechaun? I think it not only possible but probable. Somehow she survived the dog attack without his knowing it. And I never told Gram and Gramp or anyone else about the marks, because they didn't seem significant at the time, especially since Gram didn't believe me."

"She had begun to wonder if you could have been right. In later years she told me several times she wished she had taken you seriously and looked into the matter. You remember that little box we took into the woods just before she died?"

John nodded.

"Well, in addition to some gold coins and jewelry for Shamus's cache, it contained a letter telling him what you claimed to have seen. But he didn't believe it. He thought you were pretending, or simply an imaginative child. He had heard the neighbor's pack of hounds that had disobeyed Gramp's edicts and crossed onto his property. Shamus hurried as fast as he could, but by the time he reached the little thicket, they had torn her to bits. He found only shreds of her clothing, and blood everywhere.

"Shamus was heartbroken and despairing. She who had stayed earthbound with him out of love had been destroyed because of her loyalty. Gram and Gramp felt responsible, so they talked him into coming to England with them and taking shelter in the Heartwood. There he would at least have them for company. They used to take evening walks there every day the weather permitted, to visit with him."

"If I saw her there, some fifty years after her supposed death, then isn't there reason to suppose she may yet be alive?"

"Yes. They live hundreds of years in the natural order of things."

"Would knowing she possibly still lived change his mind about going back to Ireland?"

"I'm sure it would. I must put it to him."

"Do you think I might see him, talk with him? It might help keep me from accusing myself of madness."

Beth frowned thoughtfully. "I don't know. He fears humans, and human males especially, with good reason."

"Ah, that leads me back to the question of why your father hates him so."

"Yes, and it is a tale that does father no credit. But few tales about him do." She lifted her head and listened.

"Oh, you must go. Mavis is coming home, and I really don't want to endure her scolding, not to mention the fact that I couldn't tell you of father's story with her about."

"So she isn't in on the secret?"

"No. I took your advice."

"What?"

"Don't you remember telling me never to admit I had seen a leprechaun? You feared that Terry and the other cousins would go looking for Shamus, and might find him. Well, I subsequently learned that many people will search ceaselessly for him, hoping to gain his gold. So I never told anyone. Unfortunately, my father guessed. When I became old enough to walk about the estate unaccompanied, he saw me going into the woods with little presents for Shamus. Gram told me what he would like. He's fond of seed cakes and sweetmeats and tobacco, and whiskey. Of course, I was warned never to take him such, for it makes him drunk very easily, considering his size, and thus more vulnerable to capture.

"At first, I'd sneak off with tiny packages and leave them at the hollow tree nearest the meadow, since I was still forbidden to go deep into the woods unaccompanied. Later . . . Oh! You really must go. Mavis is here, and I don't want to endure her scolding."

John rubbed the knot that remained on his head thoughtfully. "I understand. I'm not sure your father will let me stay at Blayne Manor, though, so how are we to . . . ?"

"We'll trade places if he kicks you out. You'll stay here, and I'll go to the manor. I need to, anyway. I have some estate business to see to, and Mother needs me to visit her often."

"She is not looking at all well."

"No." Beth sighed. "She seems to be just wasting away. She takes a great deal of laudanum. Father won't send for a London physician, and the local apothecary has no idea what is wrong."

John scowled. "Shall I send for a physician?"

She touched his cheek briefly with her hand, then drew it away. "If mother will agree. He would have to see her here, though. Come, out the door with you. I'll tell my manservant to make all ready for you and your valet while you are here."

"Oh, the devil. I don't even have a valet. He has gone on to Scotland, where I was supposed to be entertaining guests."

"Then you had best go to them." She drew herself up, expression closed. "Go now. In addition to having a scolding tongue, Mavis has a gossiping one. You'll ruin my reputation."

He went out the door, stopped, and stuck his head back in. "I'll transfer my things here if your father throws me out."

Relief made Beth almost limp. "Thank you," she whispered. "Now, for heaven's sake, *go!*"

Chapter 10

John felt like a guilty schoolboy as he hurried away from Hintock cottage, pausing only when a bend in the path and a tree safely hid him from the kitchen window. As he returned to Blayne Manor, he pondered the decision he had made to embroil himself in Beth's problems, which not only meant dealing with her father but accepting and acting on the notion that a mythical creature was real.

As he clambered over the decaying gate between the Hintock land and Heartwood, he once again had that eerie feeling of being watched. He stopped on the other side of the fence, looked all around, then bellowed out, "All right, I know you are there. I believe in you, and I've come to help you. Show yourself!"

Nothing happened except that all the birds stopped their calling, and small, scrabbling sounds told of frightened mice or rabbits scurrying away.

I have gone mad, John thought. *I often thought I would, after the war, and now it has happened. The smartest thing I could do is get away from here and go back to my pursuit of pleasure.* All the way back through the woods he tried to talk himself into doing just that. But when he emerged to the sight and sound of axes and saws snatching ancient trees from their place on earth, his arguments vanished into dust.

I want you to do it because it is the right thing to do.

That was what Beth had said. *And it is the right thing,* he thought. *Even if there is no such thing as a leprechaun, it is a terrible wrong to cut up these magnificent old trees and deprive all of the other wild things Beth had so lovingly documented of their home, their very place on the planet.* Old woods were almost nonexistent in England. He would not allow this one to be destroyed too!

As he made his way through the chaotic woodcutting project, he tried to think how he could get Lord Blayne to stop the destruction.

He despises me, blames me for Terry's death. What possible thing could I say or do to change his mind? He had never gotten on with Beth's father, a ne'er-do-well whose main ambition was to lift the skirt of every female who came his way except his wife's. It had been his fault that Beth had been able to wander off into the woods that long-ago day, for he had been dallying with the girl's governess.

Suddenly John's thoughts veered off. How had it come about that Beth had been married to a very old man, a country nobody, a mere vicar? Why had her father, a man as greedy as he was lascivious, let his beautiful daughter go to such a man? And what had caused her to detest the thought of marriage? He tried to shake these thoughts, for danger of further emotional entanglement lay in that direction.

When John entered Blayne Manor, the butler greeted him cordially.

"The master would like to speak with you once you have broken your fast," he said.

"I have done so. Where is he?"

As he made his way to the smoking room, John dreaded the coming confrontation, because he had no idea what to do to convince Blayne to stop his destructive plan. Moreover, he fully expected, the butler's cordiality aside, to be told to vacate the premises at once.

To his astonishment, Lord Blayne greeted him affably,

even enthusiastically. "Well, what do you think of my little project, now that you've seen it?"

"Not such a little project, sir. And I wish you would call it off."

"Daresay you do. Robbing you of a mint in timber, ain't I." Lord Blayne chuckled. "But it's for a good cause."

"Destroying a leprechaun? I don't call that a good cause."

"A leprechaun? You've been talking to my daughter. She'd better be careful with that talk—she'll end up in bedlam."

"Give over, sir. I know you've seen him too. I know they exist, so you've no need to fear my thinking you mad."

"You know? Hah! Said you were sweet on Beth. She's turned your head."

"Not at all. I saw one once myself. In Ireland."

Blayne stared at him, mouth open.

"A female, sir. A fierce little thing. I grabbed her and she bit me. I still have the scar on my hand." He held out his right arm and traced the old marks, barely discernible now.

"A female? You're lying. There's only the one. He told me so. That is . . . damn it all, Gram's stories . . ."

"I know better."

Lord Blayne rubbed at his eyes, trying to take in a disagreeable reality. "Damn, boy. You do love to give me bad news, don't you." He reached for the brandy bottle at his elbow and poured himself a generous drink, not offering any to John.

"Why is that bad news? You want rid of the leprechaun in the woods for some reason. I think with Beth's help we can convince him to go back to Ireland, to be with this female."

"No!" Lord Blayne's fist came down on the table by his chair, making it jump. "No, by God. He'll not escape my vengeance. For what he did to me . . . And who's to say moving him to Ireland would take away the curse? No, I'll get him first, then go after this female. They are evil, unnatural creatures who should have been destroyed long ago. Where did you see her?"

"Tell me about this curse, sir."

Blayne took another generous pull of brandy. "Just let me say this: Don't ever mistake a leprechaun for a harmless little fairy tale being. Evil creatures, they are. Wicked! The local folk have been wise to avoid the woods. Cross those fiends, and they'll have their revenge."

John pretended great concern. "Evil? Well, I've no wish to help preserve something evil. Tell me about it, will you, sir?"

Lord Blayne stared into the distance. "'Twas on Beth's sixteenth birthday. She took her little basket into the wood, sneaking about as if no one knew, when everyone did, and laughed at her or sympathized with her, depending upon their point of view. Gram and Gramp had encouraged her fancies, of course. But as you know, Gram had died the previous spring and Gramp not long after."

John nodded. He remembered well the look of triumph on Blayne's face as his grandfather had been placed in the family vault. Gramp had held the reins of power for many years, and held them tightly, until Gram died, when he just seemed to give up.

"I went a little crazy after the old man died. You don't know about that, I suppose, having by then begun your military career. I gamed too much, whored too much, spent too much on luxuries Gramp had always denied me. I should have taken my wife's warnings to heart. But I didn't, so it was low tide with me, and I needed to recoup. When I saw Beth sneaking off with her little basket, I followed her. Couldn't get close enough to see the thing, if in fact he came out then, but I saw the tree where she left the basket, just inside the hollow part. So the next night, I went out with a little present of my own. They're mighty fond of whiskey, you know. I sat a small flask of it down there by the hollow tree. Spilled some of it about so he could smell it. Only I put a little something extra in it."

"Laudanum." John fought to keep the anger from his face.

"Right. He liked it mighty fine. I hid myself nearby. Waited in the damp for hours, and at last I had him. He drank it up and began to reel about, singing, if you want to call it that, in some unknown tongue and tone. It was easy enough for me to pop him in a game bag. Carried him home and put him in a birdcage. That 'un right over there, the one Gram used to put that disgusting parrot in."

Lord Blayne pointed to the iron cage. "Oh, how he howled when he woke up. Claimed the iron hurt him, begged me to release him. Promised to take me to his gold if I would. Oh, no, he couldn't tell me where it was, he said. Only he could release it from its enchanted hiding place. I'd heard how tricksy they are, so I never let him out of that cage, but took him in it, with a drape over it, and tramped the woods until he told me where to dig. There *was* gold, too. A pitiful little box of trinkets, most of which looked like child's jewelry, and I expect it was. Beth's, probably. Stolen from her, with her thinking him such a dear creature. Some of it I recognized as Gram's. A few guineas. A Roman coin or two. But nothing that would help me out of my deep indebtedness."

Lord Blayne paused, anger and then something like fear passing over his features.

At last John prompted him, "So you let him go, though no better off."

"Hell, no! I knew he had to have more somewhere. Told you they were tricksters. I shook him about in that cage, with him screaming that the iron burned him wherever it touched him. He claimed he hadn't been able to earn any gold here. No one to sell shoes to, because there were no fairies about. Rot! Told him he'd stay in that cage forever if he did not tell me where the rest was. He said I'd regret it, that it was bad luck to break faith with a leprechaun. Said he'd put a curse on me. What threats and imprecations and pleas for pity he set up, what a caterwauling! Well, it was all to no avail. I'd no fear of the creature then. To shut him up I gave him more whiskey and laudanum. Carried him back here to let him think things over. I figured by morning he'd be ready to tell me where he'd hid his true fortune."

Lord Blayne's face flushed with fury. "Only thing is, he wasn't there in the morning. My daughter, my dutiful daughter—oh, the little witch—had freed him. And had the nerve to scold me for keeping him. Sprouted the same nonsense about his being banished from faery and unable to earn anything by making shoes. He only had what she and Gram had given him for his safety, as he knew that if captured, he'd have to ransom his way out."

Lord Blayne put his head in his hands. "I don't know if that was the truth or not, but he was telling the truth when he said it was bad luck I'd have for breaking faith with him. Bad luck from that day to this, beginning with Beth's marriage. No, 'twas before that. My horses all came in badly at Newmarket, and I lost so much money at my clubs I had to give up play there. I was forced to use her dowry to pull myself out of the river tick."

John growled low in the throat. "So that's why she was forced to marry a nobody, an old man at that. You took her dowry."

"Not precisely." Blayne looked ashamed for a moment, then threw his shoulders back. "Her fault, really. Defiant little witch. I had no way to get at her dowry or her mother's settlement. Gramp never did trust me, the old tartar. So I set up a private card game with Bannermain, a man of title who would be an acceptable husband for Beth, but who would certainly require her dowry to marry her. Don't know if you remember, but she was a plain little creature then, too plump and face covered with spots. No sense giving her a season and trying for a rich match."

John frowned, remembering. He had last seen Beth at Gram's funeral, just before leaving for the peninsula. She had been fifteen. Unexpectedly shy, she had avoided him for much of his visit, but he had cornered her at last and put her at her ease. He remembered with pleasure their long walk through the woods. He had been delighted with her knowledge of the various creatures and plants there. She had helped him to see it as he never had before. But he remembered thinking what a pity it was that she had such an unfortunate complexion. Her weight had not bothered him much, for he liked a woman with some meat on her bones. Of course, he had not been thinking of her as a potential wife for himself. He'd never thought of her that way until . . .

He realized his attention had wandered. Lord Blayne was telling him, in card-by-card detail, how he had played against Bannermain. "I'm sorry, sir, but I lost the thread a moment. What was the bet, again?"

"A brilliant stroke, if I must say so myself. Either way, Beth would have a husband, so I'd be rid of her. If I won, I'd have her dowry too. That was our agreement. Lord Bannermain would receive her and her dowry if he won. If I won, he would marry her and remit the dowry to me once her trustees had paid it."

"Lord Bannermain." John frowned. "A nasty bit of work, that man. I'm surprised you'd think him a suitable husband. His reputation . . ."

"Did Beth deserve more, after the trick she played on me? Her own fault I was so desperate, letting that leprechaun go. And his curse did its work, too. I lost that game. Lord Bannermain won both Beth and her dowry."

John clenched his fists, digging his nails into his hand

to mask his fury as he kept his voice casual. "I don't understand, then, how she came to be married to Longford."

"She wouldn't have Bannermain. Ran away to Longford, who stood up for her. Stiff-rumped old man, always preaching such hard sermons. I was his patron, for God's sake. He held the living through my family. How dare he! But he did dare. When he saw how determined both Bannermain and I were, it was he who came up with the compromise."

"Let me guess. He married Beth and passed her dowry on to Bannermain."

"You have it! Ingenious. Bannermain was miffed that she'd marry a man almost old enough to be her grandfather rather than him, but she was adamant, so that is how it came about. Longford held up his end of the bargain, too. Of course, that meant Beth would be a very poor widow. Longford had nothing to settle on her, any more than I did, even if I'd wanted to, which I didn't. But she deserved it for being a traitor to me.

"And that leprechaun curse was at work in the whole thing, for how could I know that marrying her off that way would make Terry hate me? He left this house then and never returned. And how was I to know that within two years Beth's complexion would clear, her figure would improve, and she'd become a beauty to turn heads? When Longford died four years after their marriage, she had to move in with us, being penniless. I tried to arrange a marriage for her with Lord Vendercroft."

John couldn't control the exclamation of disgust that escaped his lips. Vendercroft was an old roué with a disgusting, even dangerous reputation, known to be looking for a young wife to bear him an heir. As two previous wives had died under rather odd circumstances, he had so far been unable to find a wife among the *ton*.

"Well, you may object, but he has a title, wealth . . ."

"Some of which I suppose he was willing to share with you in exchange for your daughter's hand?"

"Why not? She'd cost me a fortune by that time. Two! One from letting the leprechaun go, the second by being so plain at sixteen, and turning into a beauty by twenty."

John put his hand over his mouth to cover the smile that rose at this mad reasoning.

"I was still her father. She was living under my roof. It was her duty to marry as I directed her. But Beth is not a dutiful daughter! I threw her out. I thought a little period of going hungry might bring her around, but unknown to me, she moved in with those crazy recluses, the Hintocks. Nursed the old man until he died, lived with the old woman after that, and when she died, she left Beth their farm. Brings her around £500 a year—not a fortune, but makes her independent. And independent she is! Periodically steals my own wife away from me, not that I'm any worse off without her. Other times, she moves in here and busies herself with the estate management, as if I should be grateful to her for that. Oh, I suppose I should, keeps my head above water, barely."

Lord Blayne grabbed the brandy bottle and drank from it directly, draining it. "Now Terry is dead. I have no heir. My youngest daughter hates me. Well, Portia hates me too, but that is another story. I am in debt. All thanks to that evil leprechaun's curse. You see why I hate it so."

He paused to open another bottle. "Cutting the forest down is the perfect revenge on all of you, for he'll have no sanctuary, she'll lose her precious woods, and my pockets will be full of your money. Do you have any idea of the value of that timber? Oh, I daresay you do, or you wouldn't be here trying to stop me. But go to the law." Blayne chuckled. "I know little of the law, but enough to know how slowly it works. I'll hire my own solicitors. By the time you can legally stop me, I'll have every tree down and sold, and the money spent. I'll have that leprechaun's hide nailed to a tree, too. In fact, I'll be dead, belike, before you can move the case through the courts.

So you'd best be on your way. There's no welcome for you here, and no point in your staying."

He turned on John a look at once so vindictive and so gleeful that a shiver ran up his spine. *The man is truly mad, or evil, or both.*

John stood. "There is one thing upon which we agree, sir. I had best be on my way. I won't shake your hand, for it would make me feel tainted to shake the hand of one who has shown so little honor in his dealings with his family and his . . ."

"Leprechaun?" Blayne threw back his head and began to laugh maniacally. "Make that public, why don't you! I'd like to see society's reaction to it! Well, I never asked to shake your hand, so be gone with you!"

John left him to his new bottle of brandy and sought out Lady Blayne to take his leave of her. She was in the front drawing room, stretched out on a sofa that looked out through the French doors onto the terrace, toward the wood. Together they surveyed in silence the mournful progress of Blayne's woodcutting project.

"So you are going. Is it that you can't stop him in time, or do you just not care to be involved?"

He looked down at the sadly sagging face of Lady Blayne, who had once been a beauty. He remembered once again how kind she had been to him when he was a boy, when his parents had been far too busy to pay him any attention.

He scratched his chin, discovering that, lacking his valet to remind him, he had not shaved that morning. "I don't know what I can do about the woods, if anything, but I have promised Beth that I would help with . . ." He paused. Did Lady Blayne know about Shamus?

"Oh, dear. You don't pay any attention to that leprechaun nonsense, do you? The best help you could give her would be to make her give up that childhood fancy. I begin to think it a form of madness that runs in the blood."

John nodded his head. "Perhaps it does. Well, one way or another, we are going to exorcize this madness. That creature will show itself to me and allow me to take it to Ireland where it belongs, or I shall know the whole thing is nonsense, and warn Beth not to follow her father down the bedlam path."

"I hope you may succeed. Though he believes in the thing with all his heart, my husband would like nothing more than to convince others that Beth is insane. He'd have her locked up in the twinkling of an eye, and take that farm of hers. He could cut the rest of the woods, then, you see. Oh, it's all so strange."

John could think of nothing to say to comfort her. *It is all strange.* But true? If he believed it, did that make him mad?

I am mad. I never meant to involve myself in anything that smacked of care and woe again, and here I am in the thick of a family quarrel. Yet John knew, even as he tasked himself with his folly, that he had not felt so alive since the end of the war, since Waterloo, as he did now.

Lady Blayne leaned forward in her chair, staring at the carriageway.

"Here comes Beth. It is so good of her . . . Her father cannot manage the estate books, and won't trust an agent. Why she does it for him, I do not know, after . . ."

"I expect because she loves you."

His aunt teared up again. "Bless her, she truly must, for he is so nasty to her when she is here. I wish that she would marry again and find happiness for herself, but she won't consider it. Well, I suppose that is understandable. Happiness and marriage haven't exactly gone together, for either of us."

What did Longford do to her? John wondered as he watched Beth competently tool a gig up the manor's carriageway. Her maid Mavis sat ramrod-straight beside her. Beth did not appear to notice them, and continued her drive around to the entrance to the manor with an apprehensive look on her face.

"You go and greet her, will you? Ask her to come to me here," Lady Blayne requested.

John made his way to the foyer, where he found Lord Blayne already ahead of him, swaying at the bottom of the stairway.

He was blasting Beth in comprehensive, vulgar language for bringing John into the picture, and ordering her from the house. Beth took no notice of him, peeling off her gloves and handing them to the butler. Turning to John, her mouth curved in a tense little smile with a tremor to it as she unfastened her bonnet. Mavis directed the footman in carrying a pair of carpetbags up the stairs. This stalwart woman took no notice of the raging baron, marching past him as past an enemy despised and already vanquished.

"What the devil do you mean by this?" Blayne roared.

"I have come to stay for a few days. There are some urgent estate matters to look into, and mother is not well."

"Your mother is never well." But Blayne did not repeat his order for her to leave. Instead, he shouted, "You shan't marry John. I don't care what he says, he'd not come here and involve himself in your schemes if that weren't his game—and yours, likely. But I'll prevent that if I have to kill one of you first."

"I won't marry John, or anyone else, so you may be easy on that score. Now do give over, Father. It is time for me to settle the quarterly accounts and calculate the servants' wages."

She turned back to John. "Are you leaving us?" He knew her question had a double meaning. She still did not trust him to stay and help her. He needed to speak with her privately, but did not wish to further enrage her father.

"As we discussed earlier, I have a friend I plan to visit in the area before going on to my hunting box."

Relief washed over her face, but still that strange tension was there. It wasn't fear of her father, clearly, nor doubt of John's fidelity to his promise to help her. Something else had Beth wound as tightly as a spring. But she stretched out her hand to him. "I hope your visit may turn out to be a pleasant one," she said in a voice that carried doubt as its undercurrent. When she removed her hand, he found a tiny screw of paper in his. He hastily pocketed it, and watched her hurry off to join her mother.

Chapter II

John waited until he was in his carriage, on the way to Beth's cottage, to read her note. He had no wish for any of her servants—or his, for that matter—to suspect something clandestine in their actions.

It was short and deliberately obscure, so he had to puzzle over it a few minutes to understand.

> *Your projected journey may have to be canceled. My friend has decided he does not wish to go. I do hope you will visit Grandfather in the woods before you leave for your hunting trip.*

He tapped the little piece of paper against his left hand as he contemplated the note. Clearly the leprechaun had balked at letting John take him to Ireland. He frowned over the wording. Visit Grandfather in the woods. Had Beth taken to believing in spirits now? John decidedly did not, nor would he wish for such an encounter. At any rate, neither he nor she had ever known Beth's grandfather, who had died before they were born.

He closed his eyes, shutting out the view from his carriage window of the fallen trees and busy wood cutters. He could not avoid passing them, as there was no way to reach Hintock cottage in a carriage except by going up the Blayne Manor carriageway and along the tiny country lane that led to Whinton village. This lane skirted the northern edge of Blayne lands, with a turnoff to Beth's property just past the village which lay on the other side of the country lane.

Grandfather in the woods. As he repeated the phrase in his mind, there came a picture of a huge old oak tree, its spreading branches so wide and its overhead foliage so thick that nothing grew under it. It was in this dark clearing in the very center of Heartwood that he, his brothers, and the Blayne children had often made their way in the heat of the summer for picnics and imaginative games of derring-do. Beth, though really too young to participate much in their battles as knights of yore, willingly pretended to be a maiden tied to a rock, about to be consumed by a dragon until the heroes charged from behind Grandfather Tree and rescued her.

They had called the giant oak Grandfather Tree because they decided it must be the oldest tree in the forest, to be so broad and tall. Also, it reminded them of their great-grandfather, so strong and straight and stalwart, in spite of his age.

So she wanted him to go there. Did the leprechaun await him, or did she mean to meet him there herself? John opened his eyes again and watched eagerly for the turnoff to Hintock cottage, calling up through the trapdoor to his coachman when he spotted the lane, at the end of which he could discern the undulating thatched roof. It was not easy to get his large traveling coach down the little path that had known nothing grander than a gig or farm wagon, but at last they drew up in front of the cottage and he sprang down, wondering what her servants would make of his stay there.

He was relieved to find that the door was opened by a familiar face, though stricken in years since last he had seen it. It was Mr. Wister, the Blaynes's former butler.

"Lord John!" The old man seemed overcome with emotion for a moment. "I mean Lord Wayneathe, of course, sir. I beg your pardon."

"No need," John said, grinning and holding out his hand. "You've known me since I was in short pants. No need to stand on formalities."

"What a fine man you have grown into," Mr. Wister choked out at last. Then, collecting himself, "Beg your pardon, my lord. Welcome to Hintock Cottage. Mrs. Longford said you would be staying here for a day or two. May I show you to your room?"

"Thank you, Wister. It is good to see you. It's been a long time. You retired when my great-grandfather died, as I recall."

"Yes, the old lord was generous with his pension, my lord. But Miss Beth—that is, Mrs. Longford—needed me, and I found retirement not to my liking. Too much leisure is not good for one."

"True. It gives him time to get into trouble, eh?" John laughed, and the old man laughed with him, but there was some gentle concern in the old eyes that looked out at him from under the folds of skin that almost overhung his lashes. Clearly he had heard something of the career of debauchery upon which John had launched himself after the war.

"I don't think I'll go up just yet. I think I'll go for a walk. I wonder if I might borrow some of Mrs. Longford's sketching materials? I'd like to capture a bit of the old woods for myself before they are gone forever."

"Aye, my lord. Mrs. Longford has made some remarkable studies herself. Have you, um, seen any of them?"

"I have. Remarkable indeed." He looked into the old eyes again, and saw that the secret had one more sharer.

A few minutes later John was hastening across the bridge. He had kept the Blayne key to the gates, and let himself back into the woods by the gate near the footbridge. He wasted no time wandering along the banks of St. Anne's Water this time, but followed a well-known track that led him into the deepest part of the woods. A fallen tree and an unexpected clearing around it, nature's way of dealing with the natural life cycle of trees, momentarily disoriented him. He took time to examine the rotting wood of the tree, recognizing in it the model for one that Beth had sketched. He saw that she had faithfully rendered the several types of fungi growing on its trunk. Then he continued on into the woods and soon found his path again.

The increasing darkness, the spongy leaf mold–enriched soil, the lack of underbrush, and the massive trunk told him when he had found his destination. He looked up, up into the ancient branches, the lowest one now so high that even with the tallest of ladders he doubted any one could reach it. No one would be harvesting the mistletoe he saw growing there, green among the just-turning fall leaves.

He found the Princess Stone, the rock upon which Beth had once posed as a maiden needing rescue, and chuckled a little at the parallel. Not Beth, but the forest, needed rescue now, but he was a far less zealous knight than he had been as a boy. He spread his cloak on the ground and over the rock and sat down, leaning against it with his sketchpad in his lap. Beth had said drawing was one way of teaching yourself to see, really see, the world around you. The old tree was too massive to sketch on his tiny pad. In fact it was so big, its branches spreading so wide, that he could not even see it all without turning his head from side to side. Little grew under it, but mushrooms abounded. He started to sketch the nearest, when a tiny, scurrying sound led him to a more interesting subject.

A red squirrel made its cautious way around the trunk of the old tree and across the clearing. It paused periodically, in that way that squirrels had, digging at the ground, whether hopeful of finding on old, forgotten acorn, or seeking a place to lodge a new one, he could not tell. It seemed not to notice him, and its zigzag path led it closer and closer. John feared the scratch of his pencil on the pad would frighten the creature, so he just sat very still, studying it and cataloging its appearance in the hopes of drawing it once it noticed him and fled.

When the little fellow was less than ten feet from him it suddenly sat back on its hind legs, forepaws tucked closely together, and looked directly at him. It stood still for quite a while, and John knew it was trying to figure out what he was, and whether he represented danger. He held as still as he could, surprised that the squirrel would take so long to make up its mind. When at last he could hold still no longer, he cautiously lifted his hand to the sketchpad and began to draw. The squirrel remained, tufted ears forward, eyes alert, but unmoving, almost as if posing. Then, to John's astonishment, it came even nearer. One step, two, three. It looked him directly in the eye, almost as if expecting a handout, as the tame squirrels in the park of Wayneathe would often do.

John cautiously felt in the pockets of his cloak, where he generally kept some sugar lumps for his horse. Still the squirrel held its position. John felt as if the wood held its breath. The moment seemed enchanted. Finding what he sought, he tossed it out, fully expecting panicked flight by its intended recipient.

Indeed, the little fellow flinched a bit, and its tail began to lash. But after some more cautious study, it crept forward to the lump. What a squirrel would make of a lump of raw sugar, John couldn't imagine. It picked the brown stuff up, turned it over in its paws, examining it carefully, then tested it tentatively with its teeth. John expected him to either eat it, or drop it as inedible and move away. Instead, the squirrel turned the lump around in his teeth, holding it very gingerly so as not to break it up. Then slowly, deliberately, it turned its back on him and, with a last flick of that bushy tail, hopped away, back to the refuge of the tree trunk, and vanished behind it.

John shook his head and let out a long gasp, for he had held his breath as much as possible during the whole episode. Clearly one could learn more about squirrels and, he supposed, the other creatures of the woods, by sitting very still, than by charging about as he and his cohorts had done as children. Still, its behavior seemed un-squirrel-like to him, and he felt an uneasiness sweep over him. Old tales of enchantment and shape-shifters rose from memories of Gram's tales. He stood and shook out his cloak. If the leprechaun had planned to meet him here, he hadn't shown up. If Beth had planned to do the same, he wondered how long it would take her to arrive. He paced around a bit, circling the tree, studying its upper branches. He extended his perusal to the trees closest to it, growing less uneasy and more bored by the minute. It was just a woods. An old—remarkably old—woods, but still just a place of trees and plants and animals. Nothing more. He had come here on a fool's errand, when he might be at his hunting lodge enjoying the shooting with his friends instead of growing bored in the dark shadows of a bunch of trees. Then he remembered he had dismissed his so-called friends, and why, and the appeal of that alternative faded.

Clonk! Something hit his head. John tensed, prepared for battle, when he realized that an acorn had bounced off his pate and tumbled a little bit away. He smiled at his instinctive readiness to do battle. *At war with an acorn,* he thought. Then another fell on his head, and yet another. He looked up into the branches, and one fell right between his eyes. Rubbing the spot, he moved away, thinking it odd that the tree should suddenly drop so many in one spot. And was this the time for acorns to drop, anyway? Perhaps his little squirrel friend was repaying him from last year's cache?

While he pondered the question from a few feet away, another acorn sailed at him, moving sideways. It hit his cheek with a sharp thwap, far too forcefully for a falling body of such size. *I never heard of an acorn falling sideways,* he thought, glaring up at the tree. Could squirrels throw acorns like projectiles? Just then another rushed at him from a slightly different angle. He was able to ward it off with his hand. He looked in astonishment at the red mark on his palm, and certainty came over him.

"Show yourself, then! I won't hurt you."

In the direction from which the nut had come, a bird burst into a loud, elaborate melody. He could not identify the bird by its song, and craned his neck to see into the dark, dense branches above his head.

A rustle in the leaves beneath the tree made him whirl around, and suddenly it seemed as if a sunbeam had landed in the forest. There stood Beth, her brown cape thrown back, allowing her golden hair to gather and reflect all the light in the area.

"I'm sorry I'm so late. I couldn't think of a plausible excuse to leave until I had worked on the estate books for a while, and then there was luncheon, and Mama was needful of some company. Also, I had to go into the forest from behind the stable block, so as not to encounter any of father's woodcutters. Some of them are very rough sorts."

"You went through one of the stallion's paddocks?" he asked, his voice rough with concern.

"There is only one stallion left, and he gives me no trouble. It is Emperor. You remember?"

"You came through Emperor's paddock? Have you taken leave of your senses? That horse is vicious."

"Not to me. Not anymore." Beth looked around her. "Shamus did not come?"

"Would he take the guise of a red squirrel? I had a rather odd visitation from one."

"Tell me about it."

So he did. She began to smile as he told of the sugar lump.

"Shamus will enjoy that."

"Are you telling me that was Shamus? That he can change shapes?"

She shook her head. "Would that he could. The creatures of faery are not made of quite the same stuff as we are, but Shamus, at least, cannot change his appearance. No, that is Mr. Quimble whom you encountered. He has been a special friend of Shamus's for a long time, and has become quite tame around me. He doubtless took your sugar lump to his old friend, who delights in sweets." She lifted a small basket. "I've brought Shamus some of his favorites. I hoped he'd change his mind and speak with you, but I see he has not."

"No, but he may have thrown acorns at me." John recounted the acorn attack. Beth grinned. "That sounds very much like him. He let you know he was here, without making an appearance. He doesn't trust you. He is convinced you are after gold. Most humans are, especially men, it seems."

"I thought your father got his gold."

"I've given him a little here and there, as much as I can spare, so he'll have it for safety's sake in case some other person traps him. He can't resist whiskey, it seems, and there are those who know it."

"I'm one of the wealthiest men in England," John protested. "Doesn't he trust you enough to believe that?"

Beth sighed. "Since the time that father trapped him, he hasn't even approached closely enough for *me* to touch him, though it was I who set him free."

"Doubtless he fears your father might gain some hold over you and force you to assist him."

"He said as much. Or that I might be misled by a handsome man's lying tongue." She smiled up at him, lifting one eyebrow provocatively. "He remembers you, you see."

John felt warmed to his toes by that smile. A rush of something—desire, and something more—made him reach for her, but she moved back, avoiding his touch.

"Apparently he doesn't know of your lack of susceptibility for men."

"He knows. He just doesn't believe."

"Why, Beth? Why do you dislike men? What did Longford do to you?"

"I will not speak ill of Mr. Longford. He saved me from a terrible situation."

"You mean marriage to Lord Bannermain?"

"My father told you? Yes, that is what I mean. And Longford was . . . patient . . . with a very young, very headstrong wife. I just think some women should not marry. I am one of them, and since I have the means not to do so, I shall remain a widow."

"It seems a lonely life for you."

"Are you looking about you for a wife, John?" Again her smile was mischievous, and she laughed outright at his look of horror. She turned and walked across the clearing under Grandfather Tree.

"Do you remember this rock, John? How I used to lie here pretending to be tied up so that you and Terry could rescue me from the dragon?"

"I was thinking of that earlier. I remember once Terry tried to really tie you up, and you became frantic to be free."

"Yes." She looked back at him, eyes full of meaning. "It was horrible being restrained, unable to act for myself."

"Ah." John studied her as if she were a rare and incomprehensible species. Most women yearned for strong men to take charge of them, didn't they?

She turned aside and began walking away. "Don't follow me. I'm going to leave these goodies where Shamus can find them. I'll be back shortly." She pulled her cape up to cover that golden hair. Almost instantly he lost her in the woods as she strode away, her brown cloak blending in with the trees and their shadows.

While she was gone, John resumed his throne upon the rock. Before Beth had joined him under Grandfather Tree, his thoughts had begun to turn to ways of escaping this predicament and assembling some roistering friends at his hunting box. Now other thoughts crowded his mind, thoughts of gold. A golden-haired widow, determined to remain unmarried, who had briefly shown passion when he kissed her at Wayneathe. A wily rascal of a leprechaun with a pitiful little hoard of gold. Both of them wary, full of distrust of men and the fear of losing their freedom. But damn it all, he had to get his hands on the leprechaun somehow and get him out of England before Blayne destroyed him.

If I could just find where she took that basket, then I could pull Blayne's trick and capture him with some whiskey and laudanum. John looked carefully at the path she had taken. He could just make out prints of her feet here and there in the leaf-litter. He doubted he could follow her now, for evening was adding to the eternal gloom of the thick trees. But if he came out tomorrow at noon, when the light was brightest, he wondered if he might be able to follow her tracks to where she'd left the leprechaun's treats. A bottle of laudanum-laden whiskey and he'd have the creature.

And if you fail, he'll distrust you more than ever. John shook his head. That was the wrong way to go about it. He wondered just how big this hoard of gold was the little fellow was hiding. He chuckled at the thought that he, one of the richest men in England, might covet it. But the leprechaun's distrust ran deep, and with justification.

He wondered how deep the distrust of men went in Beth. But why wonder that? For the first time, he now allowed himself to admit he wanted to make love to her, that he desired her more than he had ever desired any other woman. Shouldn't his desire for her be easier to satisfy if she wasn't wishing for a husband? Her response to his kiss at Wayneathe showed she was not cold. They could have an affair. Discreet and brief, for surely he'd tire of her as quickly as he did any other woman.

And if he didn't? John felt a sense of panic, knowing

he'd flee her if he found anything more than lust developing between them. He didn't want to have any strong attachments. Attachments led to just the sort of thing he was enmeshed in now, full of problems and cares. Yet somehow the notion of loving and leaving Beth disgusted him, though he had done so with several other young society widows or matrons.

I'm changing, he thought, and was afraid. *I'd best give Beth the widest possible berth, and get through this business as quickly as possible, before I become too attached to her to break away.* Beth was not the only one who valued her freedom.

As Beth returned to the dense shade beneath Grandfather Tree, she dropped her hood back again, and once again her golden hair blazed forth. He realized why she had covered her head. She could easily be followed through the woods, even in the night, with her bright hair.

She still had her little basket with her, but it was clearly lighter. He took it from her as they began their trek out of the woods.

"Would his hoard of gold fill this basket?" John asked as he swung it up to examine it.

"I shouldn't think so. I haven't been able to give him very much, and how else is he to get it?"

"I wonder . . . If I brought him this basket, or something even larger, filled with gold, and gave it to him, would that convince him I'm not after his precious treasure?"

The way Beth's pinched, worried expression changed to one of almost starry-eyed admiration gave him his answer, and warmed him to his toes in the process.

"Oh! It might. It just might." She hugged his arm, looking up at him eagerly. "He is unpredictable, but that just might do the trick."

"I'll have to go to Bristol, where there's a bank of a decent size. It will take me a few days. Money can't solve every problem in the world, but it can come in very handy at times." They had almost reached the place where their paths had to diverge, he to return to Hintock cottage, she to Blayne Manor. He stopped suddenly, as if stricken by a thunderbolt. "Very handy! I know how to stop the destruction of the woods, too!"

"How?" Beth faced him, eyes wide.

"You are in a position to know what the workers are paid, aren't you?"

"Of course. I manage the estate books." As the turn of his thoughts became clear, her eyes widened even more. "Oh, John, would you? Pay them not to work?"

He nodded, filled with pleasure at the joy in her eyes.

"But you couldn't keep that up indefinitely. Not even your pockets are that deep."

"I wouldn't have to keep it up indefinitely. I'll contact my solicitor, start the legal process to prevent Blayne from destroying entailed property. It may be embarrassing and unpleasant for you, if it goes so far as a trial."

"I don't care about that!"

"Good! Send over the payroll information to me by note as early tomorrow as you can. I'll double your father's wages and pay the workers at once, to all who leave off the woodcutting."

"I wouldn't pay them at once. At least for those who live around here. Pay the outsiders; they'll leave. But those who live around here—well, father could just pay them more to begin again."

"My purse is deeper than his. But you are right. I'll pay them weekly, for each week they don't cut any trees. Are any loyal enough to him to reject the offer?"

Beth thought a moment. "His tenants might fear being evicted. But they are only a handful. They couldn't cut many trees."

"I'll remind them that I will be their landlord one day. Soon, if your father keeps on drinking at the rate he does now."

"How long before you could legally stop him?"

"I don't know. But I mean to put every resource, legal and financial, that I have, into this."

"John Wayneathe! You are a fraud. You are not a care-for-nothing at all!"

John backed away from her. "Oh yes, I am. And I intend to remain that way. That is why I mean to end this business as soon as possible."

Chapter 12

It was getting dark as Beth at last entered Blayne Manor through the kitchen. She left her cloak and basket in the stillroom as always, then made her way up the servants' stairs to her room.

"You've missed dinner, Madam," her maid grumbled. "Your father is most displeased with you."

"My father is always displeased with me, Mavis. I see you brought up a tray."

"All cold now," Mavis sniffed. "Been near that heathen thing again, haven't you? I can smell him about you."

"I can't think what you mean."

Mavis smiled grimly. "You know very well what I mean. That leprechaun."

Astonished that her maid knew, Beth pondered her reply. "No, I didn't see him today. You smell the woods, Mavis, and they are part of God's creation, as is the leprechaun."

"Humpf. Mr. Longford . . ."

"Has passed away and has gone to his eternal reward. There he doubtless knows a great deal more than he knew in this life. Didn't he often recite that passage about 'seeing through a glass darkly'? Now leave off, if you will. I have much to do. In fact, after I've eaten what I can of this, I intend to go down to the office and work on the books."

Mavis sniffed. "Not going to look in on your mother, even?"

"Of course. I meant after I look in on her. How is she this evening?"

"Well enough. She has retired for the night, but I doubt she is asleep."

"No, she seldom sleeps." Beth sighed. Was it pain that kept her mother awake? Illness that made her so frail? Or merely deep unhappiness. Her mother frequently "retired" early, before her husband left off his port at the table, because sometimes, before he went on to his whiskey in the smoking room, he would stop by the drawing room. These occasions were often unpleasant and occasionally dangerous for her, depending upon how much her husband had had to drink.

Beth allowed Mavis to help her out of the plain round dress she had worn for her walk in the woods, and into a slightly more suitable old evening dress. She took a few bites of meat from her plate, ate some bread and butter, and then went in search of her mother. She tried not to think of John while she did these things. She had been trying not to think of John all along the trip through the woods and pasture as she returned to Blayne Manor. She didn't want to think about John. Not about how handsome he was, nor how kind to become involved in her scheme, nor how clever to think of gold for Shamus and wages for her father's workers. Most particularly she tried not to think of how she had felt when first she saw him pacing back and forth under Grandfather Tree. It had been like a lightening bolt, the jolt of desire that had shaken her, and just as unwelcome.

As unwelcome to him as to you, she reassured herself. *Nothing can come of it. He intends to be away from here as soon as possible.*

It was good that she and her second cousin were so in accord on this determination to deny their attraction for one another. So why did thinking about it make her so sad?

Beth's father taunted her with John's disappearance, alternating his attack from "He is a care-for-nothing who couldn't be bothered" to "You failed to attract him." She ignored these sallies as she did most of Lord Blayne's blustering, because her mind was elsewhere. The woodcutters had almost completed cutting the managed woods and the tree plantation begun by her ancestors in the 1600s, when England began to wake up to the fact that it had destroyed most of the native woods upon which it depended for ships' masts, furniture, and fuel. From that time to this it had been the practice of the Blaynes to plant two trees for every tree cut down. It was nothing less than tree farming, the sort of thing that could only be undertaken by those with the ability and willingness to plan for future generations. It had been profitable, too, but would be so no longer, since her father clearly had no intention of replanting.

Soon the gates would be opened and the axes would bite into the Heartwood.

While she regretted the loss of the old plantations, especially as nothing was planned to replace them, it was the cutting of the old woodland, the one that had been there from time immemorial, that she had been dreading. So few such places were left in England. This chalk-and-flint soil and mild climate supported a wide variety of native trees. The plantations with their towering trees of a single species, all planted at the same time, shut out nearly all sunlight when mature and provided few sources of food for mammals or insects. They had been dull places compared to the ancient woods. There, by decree of her ancestors and local superstition, the practice had been to allow trees that died to stand until they fell over, and then to lie there untouched until they rotted. Birds, mammals, insects, fungi, and plants were thus provided with nesting places, homes, and nourishment. Bluebells and other meadow flowers grew in the natural clearings, adding to the beauty of the woodland.

As Beth, tears running down her cheeks, took perhaps her last long walk through the Heartwood, the woodsmen's axes rang in her ears as they bit into ancient oaks and beeches. They had entered the Heartwood's gate at last. It had been six days since John had left for Bristol. He should have returned yesterday at the latest. She now believed her father's taunts that he had really taken off for Scotland, breaking his word to her and leaving both the woods and Shamus defenseless. Heart aching, she made her way through the tiny wandering tracks worn by rabbits and smaller animals, stepping carefully as always so as not to widen the paths by the pressure of her human stride. In view of what was going on at the western edge of the woods, it was no longer an exercise with any point to it, but she did so anyway. Thus did she make her way to Grandfather Tree, as if drawn by a magnet. And there she found an unexpected sight. Sitting under the tree was a casket with its lid back and gold piled high in it, gleaming even in the dim light of this darkest part of the woods.

"John?" She circled the tree and did not find him, so returned and sat wondering on the Princess Stone.

"He's gone off to hide," a crackled little voice said. She looked around to see Shamus poised on the branch of the nearest tree to Grandfather Tree, low enough that she could see and hear him, yet high enough up that it would be difficult to reach him. "He thinks I'll come scrambling down for that gold and he can catch me. But I'll not be taken so easily. Besides, only a fool would believe it's all real gold. Ormolu, I doubt not, the most disgusting substance, the worst perversion made by man. Except for iron, of course."

"He doesn't mean to catch you, Shamus. He means to convince you he doesn't need your gold, and indeed he doesn't. But I am surprised he'd leave it here unguarded like that."

"As I said, he's doubtless hiding somewhere about, waiting to spring out at me."

Beth stood and began circling the area, crying out John's name loudly. Nothing. The birds stopped chattering momentarily, but soon returned to their busy babbling, which she doubted they would do if John were nearby.

"I don't think he's here." She walked over to the casket and tried to lift it, but it was too heavy for her. "I'll start carrying this to where you can safely retrieve it." She began stuffing golden guineas into the pockets of her cloak. "You are safe from him, Shamus, but I know you won't believe it until you have this in your possession." When she had filled every pocket and the little basket she always carried with her, she started to leave.

"Humpf. He'll follow you. Think he won't? Carry such a weight and you'll leave deep footprints he can find. Besides, that won't prove he *meant* for me to have the gold, only that you helped me outwit him."

Beth hadn't thought of that interpretation. She moved to replace the gold, but just then the woods grew quiet. Beth stopped in her tracks, and Shamus climbed higher in his tree, hiding in its branches. Someone was coming, not bothering to hide his approach, but virtually crashing through the underbrush. She felt a surge of fear. What if it was one of those rough men her father had hired? What if he had followed her here?

She pulled her cloak around her head, closed the lid on the casket, and drew back into the woods as far as she could from Grandfather Tree and still see under it. Her heart didn't stop racing when John stepped into the clearing; it just changed tempo as relief turned to something else she didn't wish to recognize. John was dressed as roughly as any woodsman, and had a heavy mass of rope and metal slung across one shoulder. He had a bow on his back, and a quiver of arrows. As she watched, he dropped this burden near the casket that held his gold and drew a deep breath.

He wiped the sweat from his brow. His rough shirt clung to muscled arms and chest, and she felt her mouth grow dry at the sight of a mat of thick dark hair at the opening of his shirt. He seemed unaware of her, and began cursing aloud quite colorfully as he noticed the casket.

"I hope it's Shamus has taken this," he muttered, "and not some stranger who has wandered in. Damn! There must be two or three hundred guineas gone!"

Beth stood and walked toward him. "About that. I never held so many coach wheels before."

John wheeled around, relief and something else in his eyes as he beheld her. "Oh, ho! So you're the pretty thief!" He strode toward her, and touched the tear tracks on her cheeks. "Had you given up on me?"

"They're through the gate. They're cutting into the Heartwood now."

"I know. I'm sorry, but it is not that easy to arrange for such a large amount of money at one time. I had to obtain not just the guineas for Shamus, but the smaller coins as well, for paying the workers. I'll need you to come to your cottage and help me sack them up in the correct amounts. But first I've got to heave this casket up into the tree." He looked overhead and then shook his head despairingly. "Even with an arrow I don't think I can get this rope over one of those branches. Do you think one of the smaller trees would do?"

"So that's what this is all about?" She gestured to the equipment at their feet.

"Well, yes. As suspicious as that fellow is, I figured he wouldn't come down here to carry it off, nor is he strong enough to do so by himself. I hadn't thought of you helping, but that will take time. We must be doing other things while your ancient friend counts my gold and realizes he can trust me."

"I think one of the nearby trees will do. He has a sixth sense about gold. He'll find it."

"I thought as much. I felt him watching me this morning, but of course he wouldn't show himself." John started for the tree Shamus was in.

"Not that one," Beth called out, fearful that John's arrow might accidentally hit Shamus. "Try this one next to it. The branches are lower, and stronger."

She watched as John, with just two tries, fired an arrow carrying a rope over a lower branch. Once he had it secure, he rigged a block and tackle and then, grunting a little, carried the casket underneath his apparatus. He looked at her quizzically, and she suddenly remembered the gold in her pockets.

"Oh! I wasn't going to . . ."

"I know." He bent and kissed her on her forehead. "You color up quite prettily. Perhaps you should take some of it to . . . wherever you take it, just in case he doesn't find this."

She shook her head, smiling mischievously. "He'll find it. Once we're well away, he'll find it."

He nodded knowingly. "I thought as much." He piled her coins into the casket, shut it, and tied a rope through the hasp.

"Oh, I'm glad you thought of using rope!"

"I didn't think he'd care to be presented with gold guarded by an iron lock." John carefully, thoroughly, bound the casket in the rope, and started to draw it up.

"Don't do that, you young fool," a raspy voice called out from just above them.

John looked up into the tree, but saw nothing. He looked at Beth for guidance.

"It's your gold, Shamus. John just wants to put it where you can get it safely."

"I know, m'dear. Your wits have gone begging, with this handsome bloke making love to you."

"Shamus, how dare you! He's done no such thing."

"Humpf. I saw what I saw." As he spoke, the voice descended lower amid a shivering of tree branches, and suddenly John saw what he had so yearned to see. The small figure popped into view and walked confidently out on the limb where John had placed the rope. Small brown hands grasped it and heaved.

"Can't you see it's too heavy for me? I could never swing it onto a branch. What good is it to me under the branch? If I manage to open it, it will all spill out."

The wizened face glared down at John. Nettled by the indignant tone of his voice, John snapped, "You're a hard one to please, and I don't believe you're an Irish leprechaun at all. Some local piskie, or perhaps merely a dwarf, playing a hoax on Beth all these years."

"Why do you think that?" the voice demanded, at the same time that Beth gasped out a protest.

"You have the accent of an English gentleman. There is not a touch of Ireland in your speech."

"And do you think I'm not smart enough to speak the native language wherever I am, then? Do you think my own native speech is any human language? Oh, I can do an Irish brogue for you," he said with a sudden, subtle switch in intonation, "with a 'sure and begorra' thrown in here and there for good measure, if that's what you want, but why? Speak my language, shall I?"

And suddenly a sound filled the clearing, a soft burbling sound like water running fast over rocks, with an occasionally lilting high note.

John lowered his head, looking at Beth. "Have you heard this before?"

"Once or twice. It's beautiful, isn't it."

"Do you think it is a language?"

"Why should he lie?"

John remembered the "bird" he had stalked in Ireland so long ago, that had turned out to be a female leprechaun. And another one which had sung so triumphantly that first day under Grandfather Tree. He smiled. "Did you use a slingshot when you fired those acorns at me?"

Shamus grinned. "Had you right perplexed, didn't I? In answer to Beth's question, I've many reasons to lie to humans, but none in this situation. Now here is what you do, young man. You take yon casket and you cover it lightly with the soft earth and leaf-litter. If you've indeed brought me gold, and not ormolu, and make no attempt to catch me, then I'll talk to you again. Now take Mrs. Longford out of here, and Beth, m'dear, you are not to come back alone."

"Wh—why, Shamus?"

"You did right to fear being followed. I marked how carefully you set your feet on the trail, and it saved you, for one of those dirty men your father has brought from that cursed wen of a place on the Thames tried to follow you."

John could not define the feeling that passed through him, but it impelled him to put his arm around Beth and draw her close. It was a desire to protect her, of course, and something more, something that made the thought of her being attacked send a thrill of sheer horror through him.

"Sure and right it is for ye to protect the wee colleen," the little man on the branch called down, for once looking at John in a friendly fashion. "There's some Irish for you, and a warning to you, too. She won't be that easy to protect, for she wants to be as free as she thinks the wild creatures of the forest are, little comprehending how very circumscribed their lives are by danger at all times. Freedom. Pah. I've lived free enough for many years, and one thing I've learned is that too much freedom is loneliness." He wagged his finger at the pair below him, then with a quick, sure stride crossed the limb and climbed the tree, up and out of sight.

Beth remained in the circle of John's arm for several minutes, looking up at the tree. John slowly withdrew his gaze from its branches and transferred his attention to her profile. "I think that little man was being profound."

"He likes to do that. He passes on to me a great deal of wisdom, some of it outlandish, some quite wise. But in this case . . ." Beth looked into John's eyes, and then away, that mischievous grin that John enjoyed so much showing off her dimples. "In this case, I think he is trying to do a bit of matchmaking, so beware."

John put on a grin of his own, not sure how he felt about that or anything else he had heard or seen in the last few minutes. *It is all so strange. I did not realize until just now how much I doubted the existence of the leprechaun.* "Well, let's get the fellow's gold buried and get out of here before whoever it was that followed you finds his way here."

John carried the casket to a place piled high with litter and humus from generations of fallen leaves, and Beth helped him scoop out a hollow for it. Together they raked back a covering, then scattered newly fallen leaves so that it matched the rest of the forest floor.

"Will you be able to come to the cottage tonight to help me prepare the workmen's pay packets?"

Beth nodded. "Father doesn't know you are back yet. But I'd best bring Mavis, for he and the neighbors will find out soon enough. Nothing and no one escapes the eyes of the locals for long, and then there would be a scandal."

"Mavis! Must you bring that bracket-faced maid?" John said, pretending to shudder.

"You are not one of Mavis's favorite people, either, nor is Shamus, but her presence will keep scandal at bay."

"I thought she didn't know about Shamus."

"So did I, but I was mistaken. Sometimes I think everyone knows but mother, and that's because she doesn't want to know."

John grinned. "Hard to keep secrets in small communities. Let's go back through the pasture, and I'll watch until you are safely at the kitchen door."

Beth opened her mouth to protest, but the memory of Shamus's warning stopped her. If the leprechaun said someone had followed her, or tried to, it had been so. He had never yet lied to her, though he freely admitted to lying and trickery whenever necessary to save himself from such people as her father.

They stopped in the pasture when approached by the stallion who roamed there. John eyed him warily, but Beth stepped forward unafraid.

Amazed, John watched her stroke his muzzle and behind his ears. "I remember when he was so vicious he couldn't be ridden, and would charge anyone who intruded into his pasture."

"He's still the same to most," she said. "If he didn't occasionally bring in a stud fee, father would doubtless have put him down by now. Shamus says he's got something wrong with his spine that makes carrying any weight there very painful. He was injured in a fall at his most famous steeple chase victory. No human can know that, so they kept trying to ride him, and called him vicious because he screamed and bucked in protest. We're good friends, though, aren't we, Emperor. No, I haven't an apple for you today, alas."

"Wait." John felt around in his cloak pocket. "I thought so." He fished out a lump of sugar and held it out. The horse backed up, stamped his feet, then appeared to listen intently as Beth told him that this man was a friend who wouldn't hurt him. At last he tentatively stretched out his long neck to lip the bit of sugar from John's hand. He quickly retreated a few steps to munch his treat.

"I think I have landed in some sort of fairy tale," John said. "Leprechauns who talk to animals, and women who do the same, and are understood."

"Shamus says they understand more of what we say than we can ever imagine." Beth looked at him defiantly.

He tilted up her chin. "You can understand this, my girl. I am not your enemy. I was not criticizing you. If I am in an enchantment, so are you, and if I am not, neither are you. We are in this, whatever it is, together."

His words and his touch both warmed her, in very different ways. She lifted her hand to touch the side of his face. "Thank you."

He turned his head and pressed a light kiss into her palm. It was the wrong thing to do. As wary now as the stallion had been, she pulled back her hand as if it had been burned. "I must go. Mavis and I will see you this evening."

Chapter 13

Mavis is certainly dedicated to her role as a chaperon, John thought. All evening, as he and Beth counted out payment for the workers, she sat nearby, frowning with disapproval as she mended sheets. She spent the night in Beth's room, and came down to breakfast without her.

"Mrs. Longford is still sleeping," she announced in a defiant tone.

"I am glad of it," John said. "She needs rest, after such a late night."

Without another word, Mavis exited the room, and John soon rode out to begin what promised to be a very unpleasant day. *And you were the one who was never going to subject himself to care, worry, or danger again.* He called himself a fool, yet felt a curious elation as he rode into the chaotic scene among the woodcutters.

As Beth had predicted, it turned out to be very easy to convince the workers imported from elsewhere to leave off their cutting for the promise of extra wages and immediate departure. Grinning and mumbling at the fool who would pay them for not working, they took the pay packets and decamped as fast as they could pack up their gear—all except one, a tall, strong, Viking of a man with a shock of red hair and a beard, who folded his arms and glared at John. When his name, Jamie Murphy, was called out, he shook his head and refused to take the pay envelope.

"'Twere himself what hired me, and 'twill be himself what fires me," the Irishman declared.

"As I've explained to the others, what Lord Blayne is doing here is illegal, and soon the justices of the peace will send officers to arrest all who continue to cut here."

"I'll await events." Murphy turned around and stalked away, his obvious destination Blayne Manor.

John watched him go with a worried frown, but soon the Irishman was the least of his concerns. The local people were more reluctant to take his money and leave off their woodcutting than the imported workers. This was not an unexpected reaction, for after all, the current Lord Blayne had an important effect on their daily lives. His tenants feared losing their farms. Local day laborers feared never again being hired to help with seasonal work. The sons of local tradespeople feared their parents might lose the custom of the manor.

John addressed these concerns as best he could, reassuring them that he would compensate them for any losses, but few could be persuaded, even after he reminded them that he would one day be their landlord and owner of Blayne Manor.

Mr. Kidd spoke for them when he said, "We hate to see the old woodlands cut down as much as you, Lord Wayneathe. They've stood there since ancient days, and some do say 'twill be a curse upon those who cut them. But we can't defy his lordship, for all that. And 'ee may bide a long time, you know. 'Tis often the good die young. Once the justices come here and say 'tis against the law, we'll leave off, but until then we must do as we are told by Lord Blayne."

John knew that all too well. He shook his head sorrowfully. Since Blayne was one of the three local justices, and had great influence over the other two, he knew getting any local legal action against the wood cutting would be very difficult. "What you say is true. And the law moves slowly. The woods may be destroyed by then. Still, I had hoped..."

"We can move slowly, too," a young voice piped up. All turned to a strong young man of some sixteen summers who stood at the edge of the group. He flushed beet-red at all the eyes suddenly staring at him. "What I mean is, with those outlanders gone, who's to know how fast we can cut trees? 'Tis hard work, after all, especially in the old woods, where the trees are thick and the bracken and underbrush trips you at every move."

Murmurs of assent ran around the knot of ten or twelve men who stood around John.

Another tenant spoke up. "As for me, my saw is broken. I must have another, or I can't cut anymore."

"And mine needs sharpening," said another.

"My axehead needs grinding."

"I hurt my shoulder the other day. I'll have to take it easy."

"Me Da needs me to help him with butchering a hog."

John grinned and began shaking hands. "That's right, my good fellows. Slowly, slowly. Clear underbrush first. Clear away the trees you've already cut. Do whatever you can do to delay. I'll go to work to bring matters to a conclusion before you can do much more damage to the Heartwood."

He started to leave, then turned back. "By the way, I wouldn't discount those old stories about luck and the woods, if I were you."

The men's faces darkened, and they muttered among themselves, heads nodding. One voice declared, "I heard of a boy came in here once to gather firewood, against the old master's orders, and promptly fell and broke his leg."

"When a poacher went in after rabbits one year, he never came out," asserted another. They were still trading stories as John mounted his horse and rode to Blayne Manor to face the most unpleasant of his duties that day.

He did not know whether to be relieved or worried to find that Beth had preceded him. He quickly gave her an account of what had happened.

"You'll find that father already knows, I expect. That Irishman you spoke of is with him now in the smoking room."

John nodded. "I'll wait until he leaves. What I have to say to your father, none of us will want an outsider to hear. The law will move too slowly as regards his right to cut down the trees. But there is another alternative."

"What is that?"

"Your father's mental state. Did you not say he refused to allow your mother to consult her physician or receive her medications?"

"Yes, but I . . ."

"That you supply them is not the point. Why does he refuse? I think his reasons are sinister. He said something about being wed to a woman past childbearing. Has he ever made threats against your mother's life?"

Beth abruptly put her hand into her mouth and turned away, biting down on it to stem the tears. John turned her around by her shoulders to face him.

"Tell me."

"He . . . he beat her severely last year. And early in the summer, she tripped coming down the stairs. We found . . . Oh, John. There was a cord . . ."

"I feared as much. These actions make his mental state highly questionable. In breaking the entail, he is doing something that is patently illegal. He has threatened the life of his wife, indeed may have tried to take it. And when his will is crossed, he rants and raves like . . . well, like a madman."

Beth clasped her hands together until they turned white. "That's the way it has to be, then?"

"Unless he can be persuaded to stop on his own, there's no other way to stop him in time. While in Bristol I arranged for two doctors to arrive at week's end. They'll reach the opinion I want, you may be sure. And one of them has a very luxurious asylum. Your father won't be happy there, of course, but he'll have every material comfort."

"I'm terrified by what he'll do when he knows your intentions. John, be sure he is nowhere near a gun when you tell him."

John looked down into her face, grown newly and deeply dear to him, saw the concern in her eyes, and felt his world tilt on its axis. *What is happening to me?* But he knew. He knew. Resist it as he might, he was falling in love with Elizabeth Blayne. He felt even heavier on his shoulders the weight of telling his uncle that if he did not cease cutting the Heartwood, he would be declared insane and incompetent to run the affairs of the Blayne estates. Once he made such an open declaration, he would have to protect the women of the house from Blayne until such confinement had been accomplished.

He realized the warning he had planned, while honorable, was strategically wrong. Beth and her mother could be in danger if he did not manage the thing right. "I think I'll wait until the doctors and their, ah, attendants, have arrived before springing the matter on him. For now, I'll only inform him that I've begun legal proceedings, and demand that he order his workers to cease cutting."

Beth's shoulders slumped with relief. "I'll tell the butler to let father know you're here. When you are finished, or if you need me, I'll be in my—I mean the estate's—office."

After she left, John sat down on a large chair in the foyer, one elbow on his knee, head resting on his hand, pondering the situation he had gotten himself into. He truly did not wish to have his uncle confined, but could not see how to save the situation otherwise. And save it he must, especially now that he acknowledged his love for Beth. Beth! His beautiful second cousin, who denied any intention of remarrying. Yet marriage it must be. No casual affair would do for his Beth. In fact, it seemed a blasphemy to merely think of such a thing in connection with her. So, not only must he convince the uncle to give up his nefarious schemes, he must convince his beloved to give up her objections to marriage.

Well, at least I am not bored, he thought, realizing that he had not the slightest yearning to return to the carefree, dissipated life he had so recently left behind, and which he now contemplated giving up forever.

When he was at last summoned into Lord Blayne's smoking room, his uncle already knew what was happening in the woods, of course. He was in a fine rage, and called down curses and imprecations on both John and Beth's head.

"You'll both rue this day! You won't stop me! I'm determined to do as I wish with my own property! I'll bring a private army in here if I have to!"

"And I'll bring in a not-so-private one if you do so. What you are doing is against the law, and I have considerable influence with the government, you know."

This brought on more raving. Blayne began to foam at the mouth and look dangerously red in the face. John grasped him by the shoulders. "Uncle, give over. You'll make yourself sick. See here! That leprechaun wants to leave here as much as you want him to go. As for curses, if there are such, I'll make him promise to remove them before I assist him."

"Can that give me back Terry? Can it give me another heir with a wife past childbearing?"

There was that nasty look in Lord Blayne's eye again. John shuddered and made up his mind to take Beth and Lady Blayne both away from the manor until the matter was settled.

"Sit down, uncle. Sit here and calm yourself." He pressed Lord Blayne into a chair, and sat beside him. "No, nothing can give you back Terry. But letting go of this unreasoning hatred can give you peace of mind. Remember, you have two daughters left, one of whose love and respect you are forfeiting by this vendetta."

"Hah! Love and respect from her? I should live so long."

"You did lose them a long time ago, didn't you, when you gave her away for a gaming debt. But you can undo that damage."

Suddenly his uncle looked old beyond his years, old and defeated. "It was that curse."

"You can't blame upon the leprechaun what befell you as a result of your own failings. You were gaming and losing long before you ran afoul of Shamus, and you were wenching and neglecting your wife long before it was too late to bring another lawful heir into the world."

"Go away," the older man said, and suddenly began sobbing into his hands. "Go away and let me think." He grabbed for the brandy bottle nearby and clutched it to his chest like a treasured friend.

John left him. He found Beth hovering near the door, and judging by her face, she had been racked by fear for his safety. This buoyed up John's spirits. *Surely she cares for me,* he thought.

"He says he wants to think."

"About giving up his plans?"

"I certainly hope that is the direction of his thoughts. Come, you are pale as a ghost. Let us go down to your mother and have some refreshments. I prescribe a mite of brandy in your tea."

Downstairs, he told both women in detail what had passed between him and Lord Blayne. "It is just possible he might see sense, but until I know it to be so, I wish both of you to leave here. For tonight, you can stay at Beth's cottage. Then I think you should let me send you both to one of my distant properties—perhaps the one in Northumberland. You'll both be safe there, and . . ."

"I agree that mother should go, but you'll never coax Shamus out of the woods on your own. He doesn't trust you enough. I don't know if he trusts *me* enough. It will take all of our powers of persuasion to convince him, and then we have to work out a method of transporting him, and..."

Not only did her objections make sense, but it also suited John to have Beth with him. She would not stand for an ordinary courtship, he guessed, but perhaps what had happened to him would sneak insensibly upon her, too, as they worked together. He found himself hoping events would not move too quickly.

Beth's mother raised some objections, but when she saw they both intended to insist, she decided to go instead to Bath, to visit a very good friend and take the waters there. "Mr. Glimley, the physician who used to visit, always brought me some Bath waters to drink, though he told me they would do me ever so much more good if I could take them fresh. And they did seem to help." Her spirits seemed to rise, and with it her coloring and animation. John thought a visit to an old friend and a daily round with acquaintances at the Bath pump room might be the best medicine she could have.

Her maid was summoned and instructed to pack a few things quickly and quietly. John stood watch as the three women got into Beth's gig. He would have footmen send their other things in trunks by cart, and the next morning his traveling carriage would take Lady Blayne to Bath. He intended to spend the night on watch at Blayne Manor, to keep an eye on Lord Blayne's response to his wife's decamping.

John slept little that night. His uncle thrashed around the manor like the madman John suspected he was.

"Get out of my house," he ordered John when he saw him. "Get out! You've no right here."

John retreated to the terrace, where he stood in the dark listening as, drunk and foul-mouthed, Lord Blayne searched the house up and down for his wife, screaming obscenities and threats. At last he collapsed in a drunken stupor in the front drawing room, whereupon John entered the house and helped the exhausted footman on duty to carry Blayne upstairs. After his valet had been roused to help him into bed, John spoke quietly to the footman, a man of middle age and lugubrious countenance.

"Is he often like this?"

"Aye, m'lord. Often and often. 'Tis fortunate for the ladies that he's usually too drunk to catch 'em, or no telling what might happen."

"Usually?"

"Aye."

John stopped and faced the man squarely. "Do you think my uncle is in his right mind?"

The footman put one finger to his nose and led John downstairs and outside to the terrace. Looking carefully around to be sure they were alone, he whispered his answer.

"No, m'lord. 'Tis more than just abusing his womenfolk. Many a man do that, sad to say. But sometimes he raves about a . . . No, you'll think me the one that's mad."

"I won't. Please tell me what you heard. You won't be the loser for it."

"He raves about a leprechaun. Claims it cursed him and that's why he's been so unlucky. Now, I'm a London man myself, and don't hold with these local folks and their superstitions. 'Tisn't Christian. But he's no ignorant farmer. 'Tis plain mad for a man of his rank, a gentleman born and bred, to believe such a thing."

"Raves about a leprechaun!" John pretended astonishment. "And a curse?"

"Just so."

"I hope you've told no one else of this, or else my uncle will indeed be thought mad."

"Don't blame me if others know," the footman exclaimed, eyes bugging out in alarm. "All of the staff have heard him. 'Tis known all over the valley, truly."

John studied the footman thoughtfully. "No, I won't blame you. The time may come when you must speak of it."

The footman was no fool. His eyes widened. "And I won't be the loser for it?"

"Not if you speak the truth."

"Oh, 'tis God's own truth."

"Good. What is your name?"

"Thomas Smithson, m'lord."

"Smithson, tomorrow morning early, before Lord Blayne has awakened, I want you to help me pack some of Lady Blayne's belongings. I'm sending her somewhere safe for a while."

"I'm your man, m'lord."

John slept fitfully on a sofa in the office where Beth tended to her father's estate. His conscience troubled him a little, but only a little, at the thought of having his uncle declared insane for believing what was in fact true. *No, not all true,* he argued with himself. *There is no curse. Uncle Blayne's troubles began long before he and Shamus crossed paths, and will continue whether the leprechaun lives or dies.*

Considering the state he had been in the night before, Lord Blayne was up much earlier than John had expected. He and Smithson had just completed loading Lady Blayne's trunks into a cart when Blayne burst from the house and stormed up to them.

"Where the devil is my wife?" he demanded.

"I believe she is visiting Beth just now," John answered calmly, as he watched his coachman and Smithson heaving the last of the heavy trunks onto the cart.

"It is not unusual for her to do so," Blayne sneered. "But she doesn't usually pack all of her possessions."

"I am sending her away."

"By what right? She is my wife. It is for me to decide whether she goes or stays."

"And whether she lives or dies?"

Blayne's blotchy skin paled. "I was in my cups. No telling what I'll say when I'm in my cups."

"Were you in your cups when you tied a cord across the stairs and tried to send her to her death?"

"Whoever says I did such a thing is a liar. That fall was a result of her own clumsiness."

"I have it on good authority there was a stout cord strung across the stairs."

"A bit of string from the maid's dustrag, if anything."

John smiled unpleasantly at his uncle. "Was it anything like this?" He took a cord from his pocket.

"Where did you get that?" Blayne's eyes widened, and he staggered back. "I'll kill that daughter of mine!"

Beth had described the cord to John last night, and he had acquired a similar piece from the kitchen. He shuddered as he looked from it to his uncle. "You will not trouble my aunt further! Is that understood? Do not try to discover her whereabouts. She will be well guarded."

"Aye! You want everything I have. My land, my woods, my title, now my wife. And my daughter, too. Well, her at least you cannot have, by her own choice. Now get off my land, and stay off!"

John yearned to grab his uncle by his neck and squeeze the life out of him. But murder, while tempting, could not be squared with either his conscience or the law.

John decided to escort Lady Blayne well away from Blayne Manor before letting her continue on her own. He would hire some men at Sherborne to ride all the way to Bath with her, as an escort. He had already sent a note off to the priory assigning three sturdy and stouthearted men to guard her in Bath. He asked Beth to ride with him.

"I cannot be easy about leaving you here alone, now that I've heard your father's threats against you for myself," he told her. "I wish you'd go on to Bath with her, in fact."

Once again Beth refused to go, and she refused to ride with him, either. "I must speak with Shamus," she said. "Father won't go into the woods. He's afraid."

"But I'll bet that Irishman of his is not."

Beth frowned and shivered. "No, likely not. Very well, I'll go with you."

John hoped the ride would give them a chance to talk privately, for he wanted to know more about Beth's reluctance to marry again. But Beth seemed to sense his intentions and deliberately kept their conversation lively and general. Much of their ride she spent pointing out to him various natural features, some of which he was quite familiar with, and commenting on the types of plants, birds, and insects that made their home around them. He saw that he could not break through the barriers she had set around herself and so gave it up. He hired a private parlor in a large posting inn in Sherborne, and the three of them ate luncheon before Beth tearfully bid farewell to her mother, each promising to write the other daily. John had already set his host the task of hiring guards, and the small cavalcade set out from the inn in midafternoon.

Beth watched the carriage out of sight before turning her horse reluctantly to return to Whintonvale. Their ride home was mostly silent. When Beth spoke, it was to worry about her mother's safety and marvel at her improved coloring and strength.

"I do believe her illness is her life at Blayne Manor," she marveled.

"It would make the strongest of women ill, I believe. Beth, I am so terribly sorry I did not read your letters. I should have come to help the two of you long before this."

"I did not ask for help for us. I only asked that you save the Heartwood."

"Which I have not yet done. But I shall."

She turned wide, hopeful eyes on him. "I do believe you will." And she smiled at him, truly smiled, a smile which shocked John with its power, and saddened him when he realized he had not seen her so . . . luminous . . . as an adult. She had always seemed to have a special glow about her as a child.

"There are other things I mean to do, too, in good time."

"I know." The smile widened, if possible. "Save Shamus."

"Well, that, too." John could not help but laugh at her puzzlement, but refused to answer her queries as to what else he meant to do.

The day was well advanced as they approached Whinton. "I expect you had best try to find a cottager to bunk with," Beth said.

"Oh, drat! That's stupid. Anyone who knows Mavis knows you are perfectly safe with a whole regiment of men in the house. And who will protect you from your father if I am not there?"

Beth frowned thoughtfully. "The widow Pettistone would probably come and stay with me for a few days. That should satisfy propriety. But she is very nosy. We would have to be very careful . . . Oh!"

John looked where her fearful face had turned. Lord Blayne, mounted on a bay gelding, stood at the point where the Blayne carriageway departed from the country lane. John reconnoitered. So many trees had been cut down, even including the decorative avenue of beeches, that there were few places for others to hide. Blayne was alone. Still, he loosened the strap on the horse pistols he had armed and placed before his saddle when they had left Hintock cottage that morning.

"I have a proposition for you," Blayne called out as they approached. "Will you dine with me?"

John shook his head. "Thank you, but you can speak your proposition here and now."

Blayne looked up, then down, then side to side, everywhere but at them, as he stammered out an apology for his recent behavior. "Having Lady Blayne leave me has brought me to my senses. I fear the loss of Terry nearly deprived me of them. But I see I must make peace with the world as it is now. I must make peace with my daughter, particularly." He forced himself to meet her eyes. She stared back, more astonished than moved by his words.

"I wronged you, Elizabeth, in many ways. I cannot undo them now, but I promise there will be no more persecution of you or your mother. No more attempts to marry you off. You may be your own mistress. I . . . I hope you will continue to assist me with the estate until I hire a competent man, and then I plan to remove to my townhouse in London and leave you and your mother in peace.

"As for you, John, I absolve you of any fault in Terry's death. It was that . . . ." A deep red stained Blayne's cheeks for a moment, and he brought himself up short. "I welcome you as my heir. You may make Blayne Manor your home anytime you are in the area."

John looked at Beth. Her wariness told him just how deep ran her distrust of her father.

"And what do you want in return, sir?"

"I want you to take that dratted leprechaun to Ireland."

Chapter 14

"Take Shamus to Ireland?" For an instant Beth's heart soared. "You are offering safe passage for him out of the woods, then?"

"The sooner, the better. But before he goes, he must agree to remove the curse he placed on me."

Her brief elation gave way to knowledge of her father's ways. "You will try to take him from us," Beth said in a low, angry voice.

"No. I swear it. By all that I hold sacred."

"What do you hold sacred?"

Blayne bit his lip, and his color heightened, whether from embarrassment or anger, John didn't know. But he realized, as he looked at Beth, that she would doubt any answer her father gave.

"Money, I suppose. It's proved a false and elusive god to me! Come, Beth. I want to change. Give me a chance." He held out a hand to her.

She pulled on her horse's reins, making it back away a little. "Change, then. Let me see it. Then I will give you a chance."

"I will! Immediately. In fact, I already have. I've dismissed all the woodcutters. It's over, Beth. Your woods are secure. In fact, I shall commence a replanting program."

Beth rode up to him, not looking at him, but out over

the denuded land. There was no activity there. No one cutting, no one trimming, no wagons being loaded with timber. Nothing.

She turned her horse back around. "I will think about it. In the meantime, I must go see Mrs. Pettistone. She is to stay with me for a while during John's visit."

"John may stay with me now. Time we got acquainted when I'm not drunk, eh, lad?"

Lord Blayne seemed sincere, but John shook his head. "I think not, sir, just now. Perhaps in a few days. But will you give me your word of honor on the leprechaun's being allowed to leave unmolested?"

"Not just leave. I want you to take him. I want to be sure he's gone."

"That was my intention, sir."

"Then you have my word, and here is my hand on it." Lord Blayne held his hand out, and John took it. Beth looked on, her expression closed.

"Beth?" Blayne held his hand out to her again, his voice pleading.

"When Shamus is safely in Ireland, and not before, I will take your hand." She dug her heels into her mare's flanks and rode away.

Blayne's color mounted again as he watched her ride away. "Damned stubborn little. . . . I offered her the chance to save the woods once before, if she would marry Vendercroft, and she refused. Thought I'd go back on my word."

John shuddered. "Any man who'd willingly give his daughter to that man would do anything. I don't blame her."

Blayne looked away. "I suppose I do not, either. But she'll see. I mean to change. I really do. Perhaps one day she can forgive me. Now, get that damned leprechaun out of here—the sooner, the better."

"Very well, but if you play us false, the consequences will not be at all to your liking."

Blake shook his head. "I know I deserve your distrust, and hers even more. But I'll prove to you I'm a man of my word, a man of honor, a man in full command of his faculties."

John felt suspicion equal to Beth's creep through him. *Did that footman tell him of our conversation last night? Somehow he knows I am thinking of having him declared insane.*

But he smiled at his uncle. "I hope you will, sir. Anything less would not be acceptable in a peer of the realm, would it?" He saluted Lord Blayne and rode away, mind racing as he reviewed this turn of events. *It doesn't matter if he knows my plans for him,* he decided. *Perhaps it will guarantee his good behavior, in fact.* He did not relish the thought of having his uncle committed, so he hoped for the best, but determined to plan for the worst.

John arrived at Hintock cottage before Beth, and decided to take a turn in the woods while waiting for her to arrive. He entered through the village gate and walked along one of the few well-defined, carefully maintained paths, the one that led to St. Anne's Well. It felt good to be able to walk quickly and stretch his legs. Five minutes of vigorous walking brought him to the clearing around the well. Though local legend warned against drinking from it on any days but May Day and All Hallow's Eve, he did what he and his cousins had often done when thirsty: bent his head and sipped from the purest, sweetest-tasting water he knew of. When he raised his head, he was surprised to see Shamus just a few steps from him, hands on his hips.

"Cheeky, aren't you. Always were. You and all the children. Don't you know that's unhallowed water?"

John nodded. "That must be what gives it its wonderful flavor."

"Huh. 'Twould taste a great deal better with that iron grate taken off. You know why it was put on there, don't you?"

John shook his head.

"'Twere the Christians, closing off one of the faery pathways. They knew the iron was poison to us. They succeeded in their strategy, too. The folk of faery have been unable to travel freely in this part of England since the Druids were driven out. Left behind some very cross water sprites, I can tell you."

"Left behind?"

"Aye, century upon century, kept penned up in St. Anne's Water and in the Drowned Boys' Pool. It always took some tough negotiating to keep the wicked creatures from drowning you boys when you would swim there. Fortunately, the water's too cold for pleasure swimming most of the time."

"I remember Gram warning us not to swim there, that the sprites would get us, but I just took it for a fairy tale."

"Which is to say, for a lie." Shamus chuckled. "As you took me for a fairy tale. Well, as you see, I am real enough. I promised the sprites that one day, when Beth was older, I'd see if she would remove the grate, but she wasn't strong enough. This is the first chance I've had to mention it to you."

John looked doubtfully at the ancient, heavy iron grate, embedded in stone and rusted so that it was impossible to tell where rock left off and iron began. *Do I really want to open a pathway to this other world, to allow access to creatures unknown to and perhaps inimical to man?*

"I will open it long enough for them to leave, but as for leaving it off, I am sure that if I do, the locals will soon replace it."

"That will do nicely."

"Shamus, if the water sprites can return to faery through the well, why can't you?"

"I told you, I was banished from faery. I cannot pass without the queen's permission. What . . . ?" He looked all around him, put a shushing finger to his mouth, and threw himself down upon the ground. Before John's very eyes, the leprechaun seemed to simply dissolve into the earth next to the little stream fed by St. Anne's spring. When he had entirely disappeared, John, feeling rather shaken by such a sight, looked around the clearing for what had startled the leprechaun and literally sent him to earth.

The tall, muscular Irishman emerged from the woods and began walking toward him, an eager look on his face. "He's here, isn't he? I could hear him." He looked all around himself, examining the shrubs and reeds around the stream carefully.

"He? Who?"

The Irishman smirked. "You know exactly who I mean. The little divils can hide in a flash, can't they?"

"I don't know what you are talking about." John drew himself up to his imposing six-foot height, and still found himself looking up at the Irishman. "Why are you in the Heartwood? You have no right . . ."

"Oh, I have right enough. Lord Blayne has hired me as his head woodsman. Now he's decided not to cut down the trees; he's going to manage this woods proper-like. Clean up the fallen ones, the branches that have broken off, and so forth. Thin it out. Pollard some of the younger trees. 'Time this wood produced something of value for the estate,' he says."

John knew Beth would not like this program, which violated the spirit if not the letter of her father's offer to her last night, but he did not intend to argue with Blayne's hireling. Instead he excused himself, leaving Murphy to hunt fruitlessly around the well. He watched from the woods until the Irishman gave up and left, then hastened to the cottage, his mind buzzing with questions.

"I told you they were not made of the same stuff as we, exactly," Beth said, attempting to explain Shamus's strange disappearance.

"What does that mean? Are they vapor? Illusion? If so, how are they ever caught at all?"

"He can't explain it, any more than you can explain how your physical being is put together and works. Or at least, he doesn't attempt it. He compared himself to water once. Said he is an elemental, whatever that is. Most of faery's inhabitants have different physical properties than we. Some can change their shapes to that of other beings entirely, but whatever their properties, they are material beings, not illusions. You know that man Priestley's discoveries about water?"

John shook his head, and Beth impatiently instructed him. "It is made up of gases. Two, I think. It has different states. When cold, it is a solid."

"Ice." John nodded.

"And when hot, it becomes a gas—two gases, rather. In the middle, it is water. I think faery folk have different states that they can enter, and this ability is under their conscious control. But if unconscious, or somehow taken before they can change states . . . We must ask Shamus how he does it. It would be so much easier to take him to Ireland if he were invisible."

"Beth, have you seen the water sprites?"

"No." She smiled up at him. "But I have seen them roil the water in indignation when their trout are caught."

Memory resurfaced, memory of times he and his cousins had returned small fish to the pond, only to see a tremendous disturbance in the water as they swam away.

John shook his head, then put it in his hands. "I am mad. This is all madness. Tell me it is a dream, Bethy."

She laughed. "Perhaps it is. Perhaps any moment now we'll wake up just as you and Terry are finding me next to the ravine, and the three of us will watch a fox or squirrel dash away."

"Would that it were so. I wonder how much of what has happened to us since that day would change?"

Beth sighed and looked away. "Not enough. Do you believe the reason that Irishman gave for being in the wood?"

John shook his head. "Blayne has set a spy there, hasn't he?"

She nodded. "Murphy will have to go, or we'll never coax Shamus out."

"I will speak to Uncle Blayne about it tomorrow."

"Good. While you are doing so, I will retrieve Gram's wicker basket from the attic. She told me where it is. It is hidden inside a larger trunk, covered with old dresses. If it is still in good shape, you can transport him in it. If not, we will have another made like it."

"Oh, I almost forgot. Shamus asked me to take the iron cover off St. Anne's Well. He claims the water sprites want to return to faery and can only do so through that water."

"He said something like that to me a long time ago. I tried my best to pry it off, but couldn't."

"It will take a crowbar and blacksmith's hammer, likely. And will have to be done at dead of night, or else we'll have the townsfolk down on us for desecrating the well."

"Ah, John. You just keep getting in deeper and deeper, don't you?" She smiled at him. "And you know what? You look much more alive and happy now than when I interrupted your pursuit of pleasure."

He grinned. "I know now that not all pleasure is sensual. Now I must teach you the opposite lesson."

She drew back. "What do you mean?"

The panic in her eyes warned him to go slowly. "Nothing. Don't worry about it. I suppose I must go meet this chaperon of yours, Mrs. Pettistone. Is she a dragon like Mavis?"

"No, a peagoose, but highly respectable. Be on your best behavior."

By the next evening their plans had advanced considerably. Lord Blayne had agreed to forbid Murphy access to the woods until the leprechaun was removed. He also agreed not to "manage" the Heartwood. Beth had found the basket, startled to see how large it was. She carried it with difficulty down the servants' stairs and placed in John's coach while he was still negotiating with her father. After returning to her cottage, they carried the basket, packed with a picnic luncheon to explain its presence to Mavis and Mrs. Pettistone, deep into Heartwood, to Grandfather Tree. Shamus had hopped down quite trustingly, seeming to have accepted John entirely. He examined the basket, which was cunningly constructed. In truth, it was a basket within a basket, so that though the weave was wide enough to admit air, it was impossible to see what lay within.

"Ayiie," Shamus cried, opening it up. "To think of being stuck in that thing again for such a time, and on the open sea, too. Still, to get back to my Bedelia, if she still lives, I'll do it. But where is the urn?"

"Urn?"

"Oh, yes! I must have a pottery urn in the basket, filled with moist soil. You mustn't fail to keep it moist on the journey, either, Beth."

"I! But I am not going, Shamus. It is John who will take you to Ireland."

Shamus suddenly leaped out of reach of John. "No! No! I don't trust him enough without you there. You must come."

"John and I can't travel together, Shamus. We are not married."

He looked from one to the other. "Why don't you marry, then? You're suited, anyone can see that. Maybe even in love."

"Shamus! To think you would even suggest such a thing!" Beth jumped up and left the clearing, leaving John and the leprechaun to eye one another across the basket.

"You do love her, don't you, lad?"

John nodded. "But she clearly doesn't return my feelings."

Shamus shrugged his small shoulders dismissively. "Nonsense, I can feel it in her. She just has to realize it yet."

"Whatever has happened to her that has made her so determined against men and marriage?"

Shamus shook his head. "That I know only in part. For some years, during her marriage, she did not come to the woods, and even when she did return, I seldom approached her. I was afraid, after having been taken captive by her father. She never spoke of it, but I sensed a great sadness in her."

"Yes. Sadness and fear. It makes it almost impossible to determine if she has any feelings for me, and even if she does, I don't know that it would change her mind."

"Would you be a kind husband to her?"

"Yes, of course."

"No beating her?"

"Never!"

"No saying she couldn't continue her studies?"

John shook his head. "Goodness, no. Such talent and insight! Though she might have to conduct them elsewhere for a few years. I doubt she and Lord Blayne will make it up. But her knowledge of natural history is a treasure. It should be nourished and encouraged. I have many estates on which she may profitably study the flora and fauna."

"Good. Good. Now, for the most important question of all, to me, and I suspect, to her: Would you be a true husband to her? I think you have led a dissipated life until very recently."

John flinched under the ancient, knowing gaze. "I don't know. I . . . would try."

"Humpf. I don't know if you are worthy of her. She knows the pain that type of mate can cause all too well, by the example of her father."

John sighed. He knew it too. But could he be a faithful husband? "I thought the creatures of faery cared little for such things."

"It is another way in which the leprechaun species is more like the human than others of the faery races. Some, though not all, of us treasure a lifelong bond, and must have it for our happiness and well-being. It is particularly important if there are to be . . ." His chin wobbled a little. "If there are to be children."

Another way in which you are like us, John thought. *Your emotions are very human in many ways.*

Shamus rubbed his chin thoughtfully. "Well, then, she will just have to take me by herself. Hire a servant to carry my basket. I'll not travel with just you." He started up the tree trunk.

"Wait! You might want to tell your friends the water sprites that I intend to have a go at that well cover tonight. I doubt not I'll make a great deal of noise, and the well is not that far from the village. The vicarage is just across the road, and the vicar has a key to that gate. The sprites might have to make a quick passage before someone comes along and puts it back on."

Shamus looked John up and down, approval replacing the censorship in his eyes. "I'll tell them. Full dark?" At John's nod of assent, he hastened away.

Beth could not accompany John to the well that night. Her chaperon and maid would have certainly objected, but at any rate, she had visitors. The current vicar of Whinton and his wife came to call, as was their wont on Sunday evenings. They felt it their duty to comfort the widow of their predecessor, and to see that she stayed on the straight and narrow path, living by herself as she did. They were astonished to find a man in residence, and only a little mollified to learn that Mrs. Pettistone was staying too.

Beth had forgotten it was Sunday, and had to apologize for being absent from church that day. With Mavis's help, she stretched a meal meant for three to feed five. John joined them, but scandalized the vicar by excusing himself shortly after dinner.

"I do beg your pardon, sir, but I had agreed to meet Lord Blayne to discuss restoring the woods."

"Lord Blayne should have finished the job," the vicar declared. "Those woods have been the subject of superstition in this area for generations, and are still, if you would believe it. Generations of Christianity have not eradicated these heathen superstitions in this little corner of Dorset, I regret to say. He should have cut down every tree and set sheep to graze in the meadows."

"I am not of your opinion, sir," John replied frostily. "Nor is Mrs. Longford. Her nature studies . . ."

"She is a young woman yet, and should remarry, not spend hours tramping alone in woods and fields."

John pushed the port bottle toward the parson. "Sir, I wish I could remain to debate with you, but I have important business to conduct."

The vicar took the bottle quite willingly and poured himself a libation. "While you are at it, I hope you will help convince Lord Blayne of our plan to cap St. Anne's Well. The rituals performed there are barely disguised paganism, Lord Wayneathe. I do not refer to those done in the light of day, but after dark. I know that some of my parishioners sneak over the gate on All Saints' Eve, and now, of course, with one of the gates breeched, they can go there anytime they wish."

John snapped his brows together. "I had no idea! I will study the situation."

Gratified, the vicar saluted him with his wine glass. John suspected that it would be some time before he left that excellent bottle of port to join the ladies.

John was pleased that the parson and his wife were with Beth, rather than in the vicarage just across the street from the gate and the well. Holding up a lantern, he moved along the open path as quickly as his heavy burden of hammer and chisel allowed. He did not see Shamus, but decided to go ahead anyway. Likely the leprechaun was nearby, and knew what was going on.

To his surprise, the grid covering the well yielded quickly to his assault. Ancient iron fastenings gave way after one or two sharp taps of the blacksmith's hammer and chisel. He was able to lift the heavy grate off intact and set it down on the ground next to the well. It bubbled up quite merrily, and he jumped back to keep from getting a wetting, surprised to see that the grate had interfered so much with the flow.

Dimming his lantern and walking several feet away, he wondered how he would know if and when the sprites made their escape. He called himself a fool for even believing in such things. In the darkness, his whole adventure with Beth took on an intense sense of unreality.

Why the devil don't you leave for Scotland, before you are mad as a march hare? he asked himself. At just that moment a sound began, a sort of whooshing such as a substantial boat might make moving through a body of water. He turned his dimmed lantern toward the well and saw that the water seemed to be flowing upstream and into it, instead of the other way around. What a bubbling and frothing there was, and above the watery turmoil he heard another sound, an ethereal singing more beautiful than anything he had ever heard except, perhaps, the music that Shamus had called his language. It went on for a long time, until he began to fear the entire countryside would be awakened, then abruptly died out.

Awed, John moved closer to the well. It now flowed much as it had before he removed the grate.

"They said thank you. Did you hear them?"

He jumped half out of his skin. "Shamus?"

"Who else?" The little man materialized from the reeds that grew along the stream's edge.

"That singing was their thank you?"

"That, and much more. You might well call it a hymn of joy." John could see, in the dim light, a glimmer on the leprechaun's cheeks.

"Tears, Shamus? Will you miss them, then?"

"Not exactly. Grumpy creatures, water sprites. But they were some company, a taste of home. Would that I could have gone with them."

"Could you? That is, if you weren't banished? Could you go back to faery that way without drowning?"

Shamus nodded. "How do you think I disappeared when that Irishman came along? Given a little time, I can merge with water, even if it merely be wet soil. Which is why you must fetch that urn or get another. We must travel with it in my basket. If any should insist upon looking into it, all they'll see is a container of earth."

Shamus sighed. "Almost I wish I had never helped your Gram and Gramp, but then there's Beth—as fine a creature as ever lived, even if she be human—and you not so bad either. A credit to your kind, actually."

John felt deeply complimented. "I wish you would tell us the whole story. I know your banishment stemmed from helping Gram and Gramp, but not the details."

"I'll tell Beth on our travels. 'Twill help us pass the time. Then she can tell you, if she chooses. If you are still part of her life. The hearing of it might do her good. You, too, perhaps," Shamus added thoughtfully.

"I'll look forward to hearing the tale. Shall I replace that grate? It came off in one piece, so perhaps if I just put it back, no one will notice."

Shamus shrugged his shoulders. "It makes no difference to me."

John decided to put the grate back, and when he had finished, he found himself alone.

Chapter 15

Beth's guests had departed by the time John returned, and the house was quiet. He crept to his bedroom, but before he could enter, he heard Beth's door open stealthily. She motioned him in. In spite of knowing that the invitation concerned the success of his evening's activities, he could not help the speeding of his heart, the warm coursing of desire through his blood as he entered her room. If only he dared take her in his arms!

She looked so adorable with her nightcap perched on her head, her golden hair in a loose braid down her back. She wore a long white shift. High at the neck and long-sleeved, it was as modest as any other garment in her wardrobe, yet she hastened to draw on a robe as soon as she had shut the door silently behind him.

"Did you hear them?" he asked her.

"Oh, yes! So beautiful. I've heard them once or twice before, after a flood cleansed their little pool. Poor things, cooped up in that tiny space so long. And it must have been especially bad since the woodcutting began sending sediment downstream."

"Did your guests hear? What did they make of it?"

"The vicar didn't. I don't think he was capable of hearing anything. Did you leave him with a full bottle of port?"

John nodded, laughing softly. "Don't tell me our good minister drank the whole thing?"

"Indeed he did. His wife was most indignant. And then the singing started, and she thought a storm was coming, and how was she to get home, for he was in no shape to drive their gig. Such a Cheltingham tragedy as she enacted! I sent Whiting to drive them home, with a horse tied behind to ride back on. I hope you don't mind."

John shook his head. "I'm only sorry I did not get to see our so-proper parson castaway."

Beth tried to look disapproving, but a little giggle broke through, which she quickly stifled. Motioning him to silence, she stood listening for a long time to be sure they had not awakened Mrs. Pettistone, sleeping in the next room.

"We'd best talk about this some more tomorrow."

"Yes. Beth, if I compromised you, would you marry me?"

Beth felt her heart turn over, then begin to beat with a deep pulsing. She did not like the feelings his words and nearness invoked. "No! I've told you again and again . . ."

He put out his hand and cupped the side of her face. "One day, you must tell me why. All of it! I insist on it. If nothing else, as a return for helping you with this bizarre situation."

Her eyes grew wide, and it seemed to him in the dim light that there was a sheen of tears in them. "Very well. But not until Shamus is safely away."

"You fear I won't go through with it if I know?"

She led him to the door, finger to her lips. He bent over and whispered in her ear, but it was not what Beth feared and at the same time longed to hear. Instead, he whispered, "We must get ourselves a sturdy bit of pottery that will hold some soil."

"Oh!" She nodded, and urged him out the door.

While John gathered the items Shamus needed for their trip to Ireland, Beth packed her own things. Because they felt it would be harder for her father to intercept her once she was safely aboard ship, they decided on the long sea route from Bristol rather than going overland to Holyhead before taking ship. John would be going with her to Bristol to book passage for her, Mavis, her butler, and John's coachman. On economic grounds, she had objected to taking so many on the long journey, but John waved aside her protests. "I will pay for their passage. You need all of them. Wister is devoted to you, and his dignity cannot help but procure for you the best accommodation and treatment a lady traveling without a gentleman escort can have. As for Whiting, he has relatives in Ireland, and would relish the opportunity to go along. He is also strong as an ox. He can carry the basket, which will be quite heavy with both the leprechaun and that urn of soil in it."

He tried in vain to convince her to let him accompany her. "With such chaperons . . ."

"Servants can never be seen as chaperons. Now give over, do. In a few weeks you can rejoin your friends and your little army of demi-reps, and you can forget all about me."

That is what she thinks of me, and why shouldn't she? John felt shame flushing his face. "I don't want to forget all about you."

"We can still be friends. I hope we will be."

He let her think he was willing to content himself with such a relationship. After he had conveyed Beth to Bristol, he would be at Blayne Manor, keeping an eye on Lord Blayne and waiting eagerly for her return. Then he intended to get to the bottom of her reluctance to admit their growing affection for one another.

They had agreed with Shamus that they would not meet with him again until all arrangements were complete. Then John and Beth were to go into the woods in the dark of the night and collect the leprechaun. John would ride along as escort until Beth was securely aboard the ship to Ireland.

He could not help but wonder if she would be secure even then. Who knew how devious Lord Blayne would be? Yet the man seemed truly to have changed. He invited John to dine with him the evening after the water sprites had been freed, and his actions were all that was cordial. He drank but little, and spoke sorrowfully of the loss of his wife and daughter's company. He and John even managed to speak of Terry, a subject painful to both of them.

"He acquitted himself well, then?" Lord Blayne searched John's face anxiously.

"Indeed, one of the bravest, most daring of the newly recruited officers. We had so many Johnny Raws at Waterloo, with many of our best troops away fighting the Americans! Wellington had no end of trouble with the untrained, rather spoiled young officers who joined then, but Terry immediately put his shoulder to the wheel, so to speak, and made himself useful almost as if born to the role of an officer."

"I should never have blamed you for his joining up. It is in the blood," Lord Blayne said, sighing. "Pity it skipped a generation. I should have joined as soon as Terry was born. I'd have been a good sight better off in the military than in the Regent's set."

"Your father should have seen to it, sir."

"Ah, well. His military career did not prosper, and Gramp let him know his disappointment. So he left the army and took me away from Blayne Manor when I was fifteen. He introduced me to the dissolute pleasures of being a rakehell to spite his father. By the time he died, I was past redemption, or so Gramp decided. But perhaps I am not. I still have grandchildren by Portia to whom I might be useful. Perhaps even, someday, I might have Beth's forgiveness. As for my wife . . ." He shrugged. "We never had anything in common but our children, and I took much less interest in them than I should have. If she is happier elsewhere, I will let her be."

John was reassured by this conversation, which

showed Lord Blayne capable of rational thought as well as the ability to accept the blame for his own errors. He found relief in considering that the military was in Terry's blood. This knowledge made his own conscience easier, though he knew that Terry's death would always lie in his mind like a pall.

But when he reported the conversation to Beth, she only shrugged her shoulders. She had been waiting up for him, concerned for his safety. She listened to what her father had said, her face hard with scepticism.

"Time will tell. We have all finished packing. I think we should collect Shamus tonight and depart for Bristol on the instant. You did tell him we were going by the land route later in the week?"

"Yes, but I sent for some men to accompany us as guards. They won't arrive for another two days."

"Father won't expect us to be leaving tonight, after you have spent a long evening dining and talking with him."

"Drive out of here in the dark of night?"

"Moonrise is at three a.m. By now Whiting knows the local roads well enough to navigate them in the dark. We can be miles away before my father even knows we've gone."

"You still think he will try to interfere."

"Yes."

"Would he go on the ship? Follow you to Ireland?"

"I think he is more likely to make any move he plans right here. Still, if we get safely away, he might follow me, or hire someone to do so."

"Then I am going to be on that ship to Ireland." He held up his hand to stop her protest. "I won't travel with you. I'll just be another passenger, as far as any one knows. I am not going to let you face your father, or any hired thugs of his, alone."

Something in Beth's tense expression softened. She smiled and nodded her agreement.

John learned that Beth had already told Mrs. Pettistone that he was leaving early the next morning, and that she had decided to take advantage of his escort to visit her mother. After Mrs. Pettistone had fallen asleep, Beth, John, and the servants went silently about the business of loading the carriage. Then, with a lantern set to allow barely enough light to illuminate one step in front of them, they made their way to Grandfather Tree.

It took them a long time, once they had crossed the bridge and left the well-trodden path, for in the dark they had to pick their way carefully through the undergrowth. They kept completely silent, a silence that was echoed in the Heartwood that dark night. No owl called, no tree frog chirped. The silence made both of them nervous, and once they reached Grandfather Tree, Beth risked a whisper into John's ear.

"It's too quiet. Someone else may be in the woods. If so, Shamus will keep away."

But after a long, tense wait, Shamus at last joined them. He had a bulging leather bag with him, which he tucked into the basket. He inspected the urn of soil carefully for moisture content. At last, with obvious reluctance, he climbed into the basket, muttering, "It doesn't matter anyway. One way or the other, let it end."

John and Beth tried to find out what he meant, but he waved them off. "Let us be about it," he said, firmly closing the inner basket top. Beth closed the outer one and fastened it with a carved wooden bar thrust through a rope loop. Then they had to repeat the slow, silent trek back through the woods, with John carrying the heavy basket. Just as they stepped onto the bridge, two shapes loomed ahead of them.

"Well met, daughter, nephew!" Lord Blayne stepped forward, letting his covered lantern blaze out. "I enjoyed our little talk tonight, John. Made me feel much better about things."

"So you came to see us off?" John set down the basket

and reached into his pocket for the pistol he had placed there. But before he could withdraw it, a sharp blow to the back of his head knocked him down. Stunned but conscious, he struggled as best he could against two strong men who wrestled with him until they had tied his hands behind his back and his feet together.

Beth, meanwhile, had grabbed the basket and made a run for it, back into the woods. She didn't get very far with the heavy burden before another of her father's hirelings tackled her. The basket flew from her hands and tumbled end over end before landing upright several feet away, at the very edge of the pool. She struggled mightily with the man, who gave himself away by his Irish accent.

"Do leave off, Mrs. Longforth. We mean no harm to the little fellow. Lord Blayne has assured me of that. But why should he leave here without giving up his gold?"

"Which I suppose my father has promised to share with you, Mr. Murphy?" Beth snorted in disgust, but she ceased her struggles. "Why do you think he will keep his word to you, when he did not keep it to me or Lord Wayneathe?"

This seemed to give the Irishman pause, but he still held her fast, and another of her father's henchmen scrambled past them and picked up the basket.

"Bring it and my daughter up here," Lord Blayne called.

Beth was dragged willy-nilly up the incline and onto the bridge, where John was tied to one of the posts. He was threatening Blayne's subordinates with prosecution for assault of a peer, but Blayne laughed. "And why do you think they've all kept their hoods on, my boy? How will you identify them? Now, let's see what we have in here."

"Father, I beg of you . . ."

"Shut her up," Blayne ordered. "Gag and tie her. Gag Wayneathe, too." And he went on opening the basket.

THE LAST LEPRECHAUN

When he got into the second basket, he lifted out the bag Shamus had put in it, examined its contents, and then with an oath threw it to one side. Then he lifted out the urn. Once Beth was securely tied next to John, the others clustered around him.

"Where is it, then?" asked one.

"Never existed," another muttered. "Told you so. Mad, the lot of them. Runs in the blood. Let's get out of here." Two of the three assailants ran away, leaving only Blayne and the Irishman standing in the center of the bridge.

"We've failed to catch him," Blayne told Murphy. "Too bad. But you'll be well paid for helping me. Now, it might be best if you left before I release my nephew."

The Irishman shook his head. "I know the significance of that pot, and I think you do too."

Blayne opened his eyes innocently. "What can you mean, my good man?"

"If you don't know, then let's throw it over the bridge." The brawny Murphy wrested the pottery jug from Blayne and held it, half tilted, over the railing.

"No! No!" Blayne shrieked, a sound so desperate it made the hairs stand up on John's neck. He struggled with his bonds, but they were firmly tied.

"Oh, ho. So your fine daughter was right. You'd lie to old Murphy and take the treasure all for yourself. You know very well the little man has gone to earth in here." He clutched the pot to his chest.

"Very well, I know. We'll take it back to Blayne Manor and put it on the fire. That will smoke him out very quickly."

"And then, when he's shown us his gold, we'll release him, just as you promised."

"Of course, of course," Blayne said in a humoring tone. The Irishman looked down at Beth questioningly. She shook her head.

"Little fellow," the Irishman crooned, talking to the pot as if it were a babe in arms. "Come out o' there now and save yerself a deal of discomfort, eh? 'Tis only gold, after all. And these kind folk will still be a'taking you to Ireland when all is said and done."

From the pot a voice emerged. Shamus's voice, made reedy and pitiful, and with an Irish lilt. "You'll not be breaking your word to me, will you, then?"

"Never. Don't I know, as a true son of the Irish, that 'tis bad luck and worse to break word with a leprechaun who has given up his gold to ye?"

The soil in the pot began to heave and work, and slowly the leprechaun emerged.

"Jasus, Mary, and Joseph," the Irishman gasped. "Never did I think to truly see one o' ye."

"I'm the last of my kind, or perhaps the last but one," Shamus said. "Now, ye've fairly caught me, so take up yon lantern and let's be off. My friends here are cold and uncomfortable."

"Not so fast. Give that thing to me." Blayne grabbed for Shamus, but the Irishman swung him away.

"No, m'lord, I won't. I see now you are not a man of yer word. And I'll not be bringing any leprechaun's curse upon myself. I'll share the gold with ye, for yer word that none of these will be harmed, but then I let the fellow go."

"You fool, there is no gold. I got all of it from him years ago. It was a paltry sum, too."

"Then why have ye led us on this wild goose chase?" Murphy demanded.

"I want to destroy that thing. It is unnatural, and has cursed me. It'll curse you, too, no matter what it says. Your only hope is to destroy it. Give it to me. I have an iron cage hidden in the undergrowth. I'll put it in there and burn it in the fire at Blayne Manor. We'll all be the safer for the death of such devil-made beings."

Beth began to make as much noise as she could behind her gag, shaking her head and rolling her eyes at the Irishman. He leaned forward and plucked the gag off.

"There is gold," she said. "Bags and bags of it."

"Bosh! Little trinkets and bits of stuff you've brought him. Much less than I'll pay you, Murphy, to give that thing to me."

"He has thousands of guineas of gold. Ask Lord Wayneathe. He gave it to Shamus to win his trust."

Blayne struggled to stop the Irishman, but he succeeded in removing John's gag. "Is this true, m'lord?"

"Yes, it is. Five thousand golden guineas I brought him, before he would believe I wasn't after his gold."

"It's true, lad," Shamus chimed in. "I've hidden it well, but it can all be yours if you only release us all unharmed."

"Damn you, Wayneathe," Blayne swore. "Very well, then, my man. Let us go find this gold."

"Only if you give your word . . ."

"His word isn't worth anything," Beth said. "Tie him up and let us go. Get the gold and let us be off with Shamus."

"I'll see you are hunted the length and breadth of all of Britain and the colonies—the whole earth if necessary—for assaulting me if you tie me up, you ugly, thick-headed Irish lump. Don't you see, if there's gold, then I'm satisfied. Half for you, half for me. Let the creature go, then. Let them take him away. At least I will have recovered some of what I lost because of his curse."

"You won't try to destroy him, then?"

"No! Bring more bad luck on me? Never. That is, if you, you nasty creature, swear to take the curse off me from before."

Shamus hesitated. "I'll swear if you'll take that gun out of your pocket and leave it here."

The Irishman's eyes narrowed. "Sounds like a very good idea to me."

Blayne cursed violently, but removed a pistol from inside his pocket and put it down on the bridge. "Very well, then. Lead on."

Beth and John listened as the two men crashed their way through the woods. They could hear Shamus's voice, but could not make out what he was saying. When they were out of hearing distance Beth turned to look at John, her distress in her eyes.

"Do you think that Irishman will really let Shamus go?"

John nodded. "If your father doesn't have another pistol on him, or a knife, or some such."

"Shamus would have known, if it were iron. If he gets away, what then, I wonder?"

"Then I have your father locked up. He's dishonorable, which is unpleasant but not a crime, but he is also obsessed to the point of madness with Shamus. I should have done it before now."

Beth began shaking, with nervousness and the cold. "Oh, John, what if Father comes back with poor little Shamus. And what will become of us, for he cannot doubt what you will do now?"

John longed to go to her and comfort her. He renewed his struggles against his bonds, but they had been tied tightly and efficiently.

"One of those men must have been a sailor at one time," he growled.

"That would be Deason. I thought I recognized his voice. A day-laborer and tavern hanger-on."

"The one who fought at Trafalgar?"

"Yes, one of our local heroes, but hardly the heroic type. Drank up the prize money he got, then returned here to make as little money and as much trouble as he could."

"Who do you think the others were?" John was less interested in knowing than in keeping Beth talking so she wouldn't be overwhelmed by her fears. He had to admit to some fear himself. He did not like being helpless, especially with a madman lose in the woods. He knew that for Beth, with her dislike of being tied up, it must be even worse.

Their conversation was suddenly interrupted by another voice.

"Comfy, are we? And getting to know one another? Good! What is that expression . . . 'Not before time!'"

"Shamus!" Beth and John chorused together.

"The very one." The leprechaun emerged from the darkness looking none the worse for wear. "What did the old monster do with my bag? Ah, here it is." He hastened along the bridge and picked up the leather bag, poking his head in and examining the contents carefully.

Exasperated, John shouted, "Never mind your bag. Help us get loose."

"Never mind my bag? 'Tis the tools of me trade, and my best work ever, too. Very important. Besides, I think it would be a good thing if the two of you talked a little longer, while you are both incapable of walking off in a huff when you hear what you don't wish to hear."

So saying, the leprechaun walked off the bridge and started into the underbrush.

"Are you unaware that Beth has a horror of being tied up?" John shouted.

"I daresay I know a great deal more about Elizabeth Blayne than you do," the little man shot back, but he changed courses and in moments had freed Beth's hands. "You can do your feet, and free Lord Wayneathe. I think it best I disappear."

"At least tell us what happened," Beth said as she feverishly freed her feet and began to work on the stubborn knot binding John's hands around the bridge post.

"Ah, well, I met an honest Irishman, that is what. I took him to the treasure. Your treasure, Lord Wayneathe, for which I beg your pardon. He immediately freed me, and when I last saw him, he was agreeing to carry it to Lord Blayne's manor, where they would divide up the spoils."

"I hope Mr. Murphy survives that encounter."

The leprechaun laughed. "Mr. Murphy appears to be as canny as he is strong. My money's on him." He laughed again, at his own joke.

"Why run away?" John asked as Beth finally freed his hands. He flexed them to hasten the return of circulation. "Why not go on with our plan? This is the perfect time, while Lord Blayne and Murphy are busy."

The leprechaun shook his head. "I'd no idea so many knew about the secret of the earth in the urn. My only hope now is that you can somehow check Beth's father's bloodlust. Perhaps that gold will help."

"I wouldn't depend upon it." Beth reached out her hand to Shamus. "I am so sorry things turned out so badly for you."

"And I. I had such a yearning for Irish soil, and even though my hope of seeing my dear Bedelia again was dim at best, I'd allowed myself to . . ." The sheen of tears in the ancient eyes touched Beth's heart. She drew Shamus to her in a hug which, after a moment of struggle, he allowed, and even snuggled into like a child.

"Ah, welladay. Someday perhaps, when you inherit, my lord . . ."

"Why so formal with me all of a sudden?" John put his hand on the tiny shoulder.

"I've been nothing but a burden to you, and you so great a man that other men could hang for assaulting you. I only give you the respect that is your due."

"You watched over my safety when I was a child and unaware of the danger of water sprites. You watched over Beth and kept her from tumbling down the ravine. I think I speak for her when I say we feel a debt to you, and a deep affection for you, too."

The tiny man's features worked a bit as he stemmed tears. He left Beth's embrace and stood between the two. "I think then that you deserve a story before I disappear, as neither of you nor any other human will see me until Lord Blayne is gone. I'll miss the sunshine, the textures and colors aboveground, but I mustn't give him another chance at me."

"It won't be as long as you think. He'll be gone very

soon." John explained his plan for having Beth's father declared mad and locked away.

"I don't know if I'd trust myself to that basket again, no matter what. Still, it would be a very good thing to lock him away. 'Twould ease my mind about Beth. He's harmed her in the past, and I feared for her safety."

"There is no need to fear for her safety. I will be here to guard her, at least until I can persuade her to come away with me."

"Come away with you, is it?" The little man smiled and looked to Beth for confirmation.

She shook her head. "Air dreaming," she snapped. "Nothing has changed. I am going to remain single."

"Ah, colleen, what are these fears, and why are they so deeply ingrained, then?"

Beth blinked back tears at his caressing tone, but shook her head. "It is personal. You had best be off for now."

"First let me tell you a tale. Come a little into the woods with me, where we won't be so easily seen if your father or his hirelings return."

Chapter 16

John took up a lamp one of the assailants had left on the bridge. The three followed the ancient, narrow path to Grandfather Tree as carefully as they had always done, single file. There he and Beth settled down against the Princess Stone, with Shamus snuggled between the two of them. John felt touched by his trust, given what had transpired.

"Now I am going to tell you the entire story of why I was cast out of faery, which is why I am here now, instead of with my true love in our queen's fortress.

"You see, leprechauns have always been friendlier to people than many other creatures of faery. I think we are, perhaps, more like you in some ways. The capacity for love and loyalty, for example. If ever the Sidhe had this capacity, it was lost long since. Their lives now revolve around pleasure, sensual pleasure only, and they can be quite cruel when their pleasures are thwarted. Like your father, I am afraid, my dear." He tapped Beth's hand.

John thought of the life he had been living until recently, and was glad the dim light hid his flushed skin. But Beth threw him a glance that told him she remembered, and saw the resemblance. No wonder she rejected his suit!

"The previous Lord Blayne, whom you called Gramp, had an Irish estate near Tara, as you know. He was a comely gentleman, handsome in that way that pleases both human and Sidhe females greatly. He was also a bit of a skirt-chaser. What your father is, no. Not that. Rather, the kind women threw themselves at, and he let them.

"He met Sarah, your Gram, there. Her father was an Anglican clergyman, the younger scion of a wealthy English family. Pretty, she was, in much the way that you are, Beth, with a rosy complexion, though her dark curling hair reminds me more of John. Plumper, as an adult, than you have become. I do think you should . . . but I digress."

He stopped and listened for a few moments. The chatter of the night creatures reassured him, so he went on. "He loved her, indeed he did, for to think of marrying one with so little in the way of dowry or status is unusual among your people, I understand."

The two people beside him nodded.

"But he hadn't quite given up his interest in other females, and she feared to marry him. She thought he might be an unfaithful husband. Not only was such a thing undesirable to her because of her strict religious background, but it also disgusted her in a deep, bred-in-the-bone way that some human beings feel. Both male and female, but mostly female, I fear. It is another characteristic we leprechauns share with some members of your race.

"She had refused him and I found her crying. I learned of the situation, and told her how she might test him. I knew, you see, that he had caught the eye of our faery queen. She had mentioned plans to seduce him on what you call All Hallow's Eve, or Halloween. It is a good time for the people of faery to be abroad in the world, because of your people's superstitions about that time, superstitions we all tried to foster by various little tricks from time to time.

"I instructed your great—may I just call her Sarah?

Gram has always seemed so undignified for her, as Gramp was for her husband, David."

They nodded, and Beth urged him to continue.

"I told Sarah to be at the place where the queen meant to present herself to David. The queen is beautiful. Beyond anything any mortal man can imagine, though very much like a mortal female in form. He, with his liking for women, would be an easy target for her seduction, she thought, and Sarah thought so too. So I told her that if David truly loved her, he would lose interest in the Sidhe queen if his true love touched his hand. If his love was not true, he would ignore her touch, or shake her off, and leave with the queen for a pleasant rendezvous."

Shamus grimaced. "If he had done so, he might have returned the next day, or the queen might have decided to keep him by her side for many years, if he pleased her, sending him back only when he at last grew old and useless to her.

"Though Sarah agreed at once to go to the rendezvous and try to save her beloved, she was afraid, and rightly so, for the faery queen can be dangerous to humans if she wishes. I promised her I'd take the queen's anger on myself."

"Ah. I begin to see . . ." Beth gave the little man a hug.

"Yes. At the appointed time, David rode along his accustomed route home from a tavern where a pretty wench flirted with him and—ah, shall we say, filled his hours—until he could marry his true love. At least, so he told himself, having promised Sarah he could and would be faithful to her once they married.

"The queen stepped into his path, dressed in a filmy robe that showed all her charms, and enticed him from his horse. They had speech, she wound her arms around him and kissed him, and began to lead him to one of the secret entrances to her kingdom. That is when Sarah appeared. David was shocked, and torn. A woman more beautiful than any he could ever have imagined was

THE LAST LEPRECHAUN

beckoning to him seductively. The sweet, ordinarily pretty girl he loved was calling him back. While he hesitated, I urged Sarah forward. She rushed to him and took his hand in hers."

The leprechaun was silent for a moment, remembering. John and Beth did not need him to tell them what happened, for if the faery queen had seduced their ancestor, they wouldn't be sitting here in the Heartwood hearing the tale.

But Shamus began again. "At her touch, John shuddered as if some force had coursed through him. Whether it was the faery queen seeking to exert some power on him, or the painful struggle of giving up his wickeder self, I do not know. I do know that he turned to Sarah and took her in his arms, kissing her soundly. Then he bowed to the queen and thanked her for favoring him, but told her that he was bound to another.

"The queen looked daggers at your great-grandmother, but I stepped in between them and told her plainly that she'd no business consorting with the sons of man, that it never led to any good."

Once again John voiced his gratitude. "You saved our entire family, along with their love."

"Perhaps I did. My only purpose was to help the girl who had befriended me. At any rate, I tried to mollify the queen. I made her a very pretty speech, trying to convince her that my interference had been in her interests, but her fury was great. She banished me from faery. 'If you like the sons of man so well,' she said, 'live among them. Live among them forever, or at least until they kill you, for most of them will not be your friends.' As if I didn't know that.

"I bowed my head and accepted her banishment. By this time a great many from faery had gathered around, and among them my Bedelia. She came to my side, and I thrust her away. 'You've no cause to banish my mate,' said I, and to my surprise, the queen agreed."

"Bedelia may come and go as she pleases," she said. "But you—never!"

Shamus put his head in his hands and the two knew that he was weeping. They both stroked and patted him, trying to comfort him.

"When Bedelia heard this, she said that she banished herself, for she would not desert me. We lived a precarious existence. No faery food, and the food in this realm is pleasant but not as nourishing, and dangerous to gather. No more gold, as we had no way to sell our shoes to the creatures of faery, who were forbidden to have commerce with us. No protection except our ability to absorb into moist earth, and that proved inadequate protection for my dearest, for it takes a few minutes, as you know. I was foraging for mushrooms when I heard the dogs, and the shriek she made. I ran to the place. David was there, whipping them off. His grief was as great as mine, almost. All that was left of her was . . . blood, and a bit of the cloth of her cloak."

Shamus sighed. "So you see why I doubt so much that you saw her when you say you did. 'Twas two generations later. I'd long since come here with Sarah and David, since I had no one in Ireland to hold me there.

"David promised to protect me, and fortunately the Heartwood was already protected, in a sense, by both your system of entail and local superstition. I came to England in 1744. You visited Ireland in 1798, and say you saw a female leprechaun there. But Bedelia and I were the last two. I think it was your imagination, after hearing Sarah's stories."

John shook his head. "I don't think so. Did Beth show you the drawing she made, after I described the scars on the being I saw?"

Shamus shook his head. "I didn't want to look. I was afraid to hope."

"Well, I believe that your mate survived that attack somehow. That is why we have to get you back to Ireland."

Shamus struggled to his feet. "Until your uncle is either dead or close-confined, I shall remain hidden, even from the two of you. When you wish to summon me, come on three separate occasions, and leave a gift in three separate places. Beth knows where. After the third, I will find you when you are visiting in Heartwood."

They agreed to this plan and sadly watched him as he clambered up the tree.

Suddenly Beth called out, "Shamus, couldn't Bedelia climb trees as well as you? Why didn't she climb up into one of those in the thicket?"

Shamus paused and looked down at them. His voice ravaged with pain, he replied, "She was heavy with child then. Triplets, as is usual for our kind. She would have been too slow." He hastened out of sight, and Beth turned into John's comforting arms and sobbed at the sadness of the tale.

"And yet, somehow she did survive," John murmured into her ear. "All is not yet lost."

She stayed in his arms a long time, even after her weeping had subsided into little hiccups. Even through their heavy cloaks, John felt the feminine outlines of her body pressed against his, and desire coursed through him. He carefully, tenderly lifted her head by one finger under the chin. She did not draw away, so he kissed her, ever so gently, on the lips. He kept the kiss brief, then looked into her eyes in the dimness barely illuminated by lantern and faint moonlight.

"I love you, Beth Blayne. Will you marry me?"

She froze, except for the expression on her face, which shifted to panic and fear. "I can never be any man's wife again, John. Most particularly not yours."

"If it is because you think I will not be true to you, let me tell you it is not so. I am done with my rakehell ways."

"I wonder if you are? But that is not my only reason." She stood and picked up the lantern. "We had best go back to the cottage and tell our servants to put up the carriage and go to bed. They must be worried about us by now."

"Not until you tell me why." John seized her and turned her around. "I deserve to know why!"

"It wouldn't change anything. I doubt I shall be able to look you in the eyes after you have heard it. Certainly you won't want me for a wife."

"Let me be the judge of that."

Beth felt the pull of his strong will, and her own growing affection for him.

"You know of the card game?"

"Your father wagered with Lord Bannermain, with marriage to you with or without dowry being the stakes. And Longford saved you by marrying you himself. I suspect he turned out to be brutal to you. A man who preached such fiery sermons . . ."

She shook her head vigorously. "Mr. Longford loved me. He was so kind. He waited for quite a while before humbly and tentatively asked me if I was ready to be his wife."

"He must have been seventy," John growled. "One would think . . ."

"He was capable, and eager. How could I deny him what was his by right, after the horrible fate he had saved me from? But I could never return his affection. I never refused him, and he never suspected how much I loathed our marital relations. He made few demands on me, really. Only once a week. Yet I grew to dread those nights. I . . . I drank a little laudanum before, and chewed mint leaves so he couldn't tell."

"Laudanum?"

"It hurt!" She reared back, indignant. "It hurt, always. Not just the first time, or the second, but each time he came to me. Thank God it only lasted a few minutes, but still, it always hurt! I loathe the marital act by which men set so much store. John! You could not be celibate, nor can I in good conscience ask you to. But neither can I go through a lifetime of submitting to such agony! I . . . I am not wife material, John, and so you must see. Now let us return to the cottage before I am found to have spent this long time alone with you and am disgraced. Right now I have a home, the respect of the people who live nearby, and a meaningful work to keep me occupied. I am deeply grateful to you for . . ."

John abruptly cut her off by pulling her to him and kissing her. She stiffened, offering him passive but determined resistance. At first it was the same gentle kiss which he had given her a few minutes earlier. But he let his lips play on hers, moistening them with his tongue and then rubbing them back and forth in the most sensuous, seductive way he knew.

Her resistance was strong, but ultimately she relaxed and let him kiss her, even allowed the stroke of his tongue along her inner lips. This evoked a promising moan, and he pulled away from her, eyes shining.

"Did Longford ever kiss you like that?"

She shook her head. "He only ever pecked me on the cheek or gave me a brief salute on the mouth. But that doesn't say anything to the matter."

"Yes, it does." John lowered his head again, and rained kisses along her cheeks, her nose, teased the edges of her mouth, and at last coaxed her to open fully to him. Passion rose in him, and he knew she returned it. He kept their bodies sufficiently apart so as not to alarm her with his reaction to their kisses. Slowly, ever so slowly, he would initiate her into the art of making love. For tonight, kisses would be enough.

When she clung to him, breathing heavily, while he kissed her neck and earlobes, he whispered, "I do think it is time to go back home, my love. There I will say good night to you in the most proper way imaginable, and you will go to your bed, where I hope you will think on the difference between my kisses and Longford's. Perhaps you will realize that my love-making will be as different." She leaned against him, looking dazed, and John took encouragement from the fact that she did not argue. He picked up the lantern, and began to lead her through the woods.

They had not gone far when they heard the unearthly sound.

Beth drew in her breath in deep alarm. "Shamus? But he doesn't sound like that, unless... he must be injured!"

"I don't think it is Shamus. It sounds a little like the water sprites."

"Only a little. Too musical. Too low."

John agreed. "It has a compelling quality to it, doesn't it? It seems to be coming from the well. Look, Beth, there may be danger in this. Go to the cottage, and I will..."

She jerked her arm from his and started back through the woods, toward the well. He caught up with her and they went side by side as fast as they could go. In the meadow around St. Anne's Well they could see clearly, and not just because of the moonlight. An unearthly glow was emitting from the well itself.

Chapter 17

They halted as one, staring at the glowing well with the otherworldly sounds emitting from it. John did not know what to do. Beth looked as lost, as dumfounded as he did.

"The water sprites. They want out," she whispered.

"But should we let them? It might even be some other creature from faery. Who, what are they? Shamus said the Sidhe could be cruel, sometimes, and dangerous to man."

As they tried to decide what to do, a familiar voice called to them, and in the strange light they saw Shamus hurrying toward them. He jumped across the little stream and motioned them toward the well.

"Open it, will you, John? Quickly, quickly. 'Tis the queen of faery herself."

"But what is her purpose? Has she come to help you, or to destroy you, or us?"

"The sprites have told her of my dilemma, and she has come to speak with me. That is all I know." He raised his voice in that music he called his language, and an answering sound satisfied him. He nodded briskly. "She has guaranteed no harm to either of you. Please, John. Oh, Beth, my beloved girl, persuade him, won't you?

Beth looked up at John. "Will you?"

He handed her the lantern and approached the well, which abruptly ceased to glow, and burbled quietly like a well-behaved spring. The sound ceased, too, leaving a silence almost as eerie as the music that had preceded it. He took hold of the grate with both hands and gave a mighty tug. Because he had loosened it before, it came off so abruptly he lost his balance and fell back, dropping the grate as he fell.

Out of the well came a great stream of light, of many colors, and the rise and fall of many voices in the most beautiful, the most ethereal sounds he had ever heard. The lights separated and swooped around the clearing and into the wood, then back again. As they settled toward earth, they began to assume shapes, and one of the shapes materialized directly astride John, preventing his rising. It was the most beautiful woman he had ever seen. She leaned over him and studied him, her eyes alight with interest.

She reached her hand down to him. "Allow me to help you up, Lord Wayneathe," she said in a low, throaty voice. He took her outstretched hand and felt a surge of desire rush through him. It was unwelcome to him, and he immediately removed his hand from hers. Scooting backwards, he rose to his feet without assistance.

She frowned and turned around, glaring at Shamus, who stood close by.

John looked around for Beth, and did not immediately see her. Glowing, glittering people of various sizes, several as large or larger than he, filled the clearing. One of them, a man as handsome of face as he was well formed, stood close to Beth. John strode forward, intending to rescue her, and found her gazing bemusedly into the face of a blond male who resembled a Greek god. Far from desiring rescue, she seemed charmed by the blond who bent and kissed her hand tenderly.

"That will do," John shouted, reaching for her.

"John," he heard Shamus calling him desperately. "Steady, lad. Let me introduce you to our distinguished guests."

He made the introductions, and the faery queen and the magnificent blond Sidhe flirted with him and Beth some more, seeking to lure them both to join them in the land of faery. They described the pleasures that awaited them, without care or worry.

"A life of endless sensual pleasure," Beth said, looking archly at John. "That should be very much to your liking."

"You will like it too, my lady-love," the angelic blond crooned, putting his arm around her waist.

Alarm that she might succumb to the faery's seduction surged through John. Remembering Shamus's story about Gram and Gramp, he took her hand and pulled her to him. "It is you, and only you, that I want! And you want me, whether you know it or not!"

At his touch, Beth felt a connection so powerful it shook her to the core. She looked up at him in wonder, and leaned into his embrace. With a sigh of relief and joy, John wrapped his arms around her.

At the sight, the queen turned on Shamus.

"Been telling secrets again. You haven't learned your lesson, I see."

Shamus drew himself up. "You promised you would do them no harm. I am the last of my kind. Destroy me if you will, but leave these two alone. You are the one who hasn't learned her lesson. Those who are of a nature to be truly mated are only happy when they are. You cannot offer them anything they want or need. I was truly mated once, alas, so I know whereof I speak. I gave you good advice once before, your majesty."

Beth shuddered at the cold fury that swept over the queen's face, but after a terrible moment of suspense, she nodded.

"Yes, leave the humans alone. I think it may have been

good advice." For a moment the queen looked almost sad, but that too passed, and she drew herself up and wrapped her gauzy robes around her.

"Tell me, what do you mean, you *once* were truly mated? Did you lose your love for Bedelia? Is that why you left her to come to England? And if so, why do you wish to return, for the water sprites told me you do?"

"Leave her? Never! Upon my life, never! I left Ireland because she was dead, or so I believed. This young man says he saw her after I left, so I wished to return to see if I could find her."

The queen stared down at him. "You don't know, then?"

"Know?"

"She is alive and well, and has presented you with three young ones. They are safe with me in faery."

Shamus pressed his hands to his wrinkled cheeks, where tears trickled down. "How can this be? I saw the dogs chase her, found bits of her cloak, and her blood soaked the earth."

"She was not banished from faery; her choice to remain with you in the realm of man was her own. In her distress she called out to us, and was instantly returned to faery. Even with all my healing arts, it took her a great while to recover, and then she sought you, though I tried to dissuade her. She made brief, repeated trips to your former abode hoping to find you, but could not stay long each time, as she had the little ones to think of."

"It is more than I could ever have dreamed of, to know that she is safe and we have children!" Shamus began to weep outright.

Beth knelt by him and held him. "I am so very happy for you."

"It is a moment of great joy." Yet he seemed sad. "I only wish . . . Your majesty, I don't wish her to return to live with me in the realm of man with all its dangers, but

I wonder if I might see her, look on her dear face once again? If I might once behold my children?"

Instead of replying, the queen moved regally past him and touched something that lay in the grass with her toe. "What is this?"

Shamus tugged free of Beth and ran over to his sack. "It contains the tools of my trade, though I've had little need of them these last years. It also contains my finest work ever. I intended it as a gift, a peace offering to you."

"Well, let us see it, then."

Shamus lifted out a small package from the pack and opened it up. Within it lay one exquisite boot, of the palest leather Beth had ever seen.

"Unborn fawn, your majesty. Yon young woman's grandfather gave it to me. Taken as our law prescribes, after the natural death of the mother."

The queen took the object from him reverently. "I haven't had any new footwear since . . . for a long time." She made a motion, and one of her courtiers knelt on one leg so she could sit on his knee. She shed the boot she wore, which Beth thought did indeed look somewhat the worse for wear, and reverently put on the one Shamus had made.

"'Tis a perfect fit."

"I have your size right here, your majesty," Shamus said, smiling proudly and tapping his head.

"Where is the other?"

"Ah, well." Shamus turned away from her, his shoulders hunched as if in shame. This brought him into position for Beth, still kneeling, to see his eyes. They were alive with that canny, mischievous intelligence she had so often seen there.

"You see, your majesty, I haven't finished it. Making such a boot is not the work of a moment, and conditions here have not allowed me much time to do more than survive. I have the materials to complete it, but . . ."

"I see." The queen stood, lifted her skirts, and examined the boot from all sides, swinging her ankle this way and that. She glanced at Beth, a question in her eyes.

"Exquisite, your majesty," Beth ventured.

"Indeed. I suppose you expect me to allow you to return to faery so you can finish the other one," she asked Shamus, a little anger in her voice.

"If it please you, majesty." Shamus was the very picture of humility.

"It must please me, I suppose. Without a shoemaker we are all beginning to feel the pinch, as it were." Her courtiers laughed excessively for such a little joke; she silenced them with a glance.

"Of course, we have the three young ones coming along."

"Aye, your majesty. In another century, with Bedelia's tutelage, I doubt not they can begin the craft."

"You are an impudent creature. You know Bedelia never made boots. As with all female leprechauns, slippers are her craft, embroidered with gold and silver thread. Beautiful things, too, but not sturdy footwear. Two of the children are boys. Who will teach them boot making? And they'll never be happy if they don't learn. You leprechauns! You must have employment! Always you were more of earth than faery, sharing the oddest traits with the sons of man who drove us into our fortresses."

She gestured to the whole group, throwing her arms up in surrender. "One lasting love! Enjoying work instead of dancing and singing and making merry all day, every day! Odd, very odd. But useful, too."

She looked down at Shamus. "Very well. You may come with us. As you knew all along, you rascal."

The queen turned and looked at John. "You are a pleasure-loving man, I am sure, and I can show you pleasures you hardly dream of. My invitation stands."

"My pleasure will be taken with the woman I love."

He reached for Beth's hand, and she clasped it firmly, once again feeling that sensation coursing through her that was half desire, half power—the power, she instinctively knew, that came from being truly united with another being whom she loved with all her heart. She rose to her feet with his assistance.

"Very well then. Say your goodbyes, Shamus." The queen let her glance sweep the forest. "I admit I wish I might visit this place in light of day. How it reminds me of former times, of our great woodlands before man came."

"Once a certain matter has been taken care of, you are welcome to visit here any time, your majesty. No dogs will roam Heartwood, no humans either, if you do not wish it, while you visit."

"You have authority here?"

John's jaw tightened in a grimace of distaste. "Not now, but I will soon. When it is safe, I will remove that iron grate once and for all. My family has kept this woodland pristine for almost seven hundred years, and I pledge to continue to do so. I will train my children in the same determination, for the sake of the wild creatures who dwell here, and for you and the other faery folk."

"Hmmm. You may have a hard time doing that. Others of your race literally tear the earth apart to get the minerals out of it, and send poisons into the water thereby. The creatures of faery cannot live with poisoned air and water."

"You speak of coal mines and lead and tin and . . . I know. Mankind needs these things, but somehow we—Beth and I—will devote ourselves to trying to prevent the spoilage of earth as much as possible, though my power is limited to persuasion everywhere else but on my own lands."

"Good. Your people would do well to realize that what poisons their land, the water, and the wild creatures who live there, poisons them too, eventually. Now, say your goodbyes, Shamus. Dawn approaches, and we must away. Bedelia eagerly awaits you."

With John standing a few feet behind her, waiting his turn to bid Shamus farewell, Beth knelt down to give Shamus a last hug, tears streaming down her cheeks. "I will miss you, old friend, but I am so very happy to know you are not the last leprechaun, after all."

As she embraced him, a shout from deep in the woods made her look up. Movement at the edge of the trees caught her eye, and then she heard the unmistakable sound of a shotgun being cocked. She shuddered at seeing her father racing toward them, gun upraised. At the same moment, John saw what was happening, and shouted a warning. Beth grabbed Shamus and swung him around so that her body would shield him. Before she could completely cover him, the gun discharged.

The force of the blast knocked her down, and she lay stunned, listening as John raced past her and kicked the weapon from her father's hands. She heard several blows being landed, and lifted her head, looking toward the struggle just in time to see her father fall hard, knocked cold.

John then raced back toward Beth, kneeling on the ground beside her.

"Beth. Oh, my darling Beth, are you badly hurt?"

She let him help her sit up. "I don't think so. It was only bird shot. My cloak stopped most of it." She turned around, feeling for the small form that had lain prostrate beneath her.

"Shamus! Shamus!"

The leprechaun moaned. John helped him sit up, and looked around. The sky was lightening; dawn was nearly upon them. Except for a trickle of blood on his forehead, Shamus seemed unhurt. They were alone in the meadow. The well burbled as usual.

"They . . . they've left you!"

"Of course they have. Had no choice. John, were it not for your shout of warning, many more would lie dying here."

"Dying?" John thought that an exaggeration, considering the shotgun had only fired birdshot.

"But why did they not take you with them? The queen promised."

"I have some of your father's shot buried in my head and neck. I can feel the poison working on me now. Cannot enter faery with lead in me. Dying..." He sounded weaker, and lay back against John's supporting arm.

"We'll have to cut it out, and quickly." John took out a knife he always kept in his boot.

"Not with that! It will kill him for sure."

The three looked up. Looming over them was the faery queen, her voice vibrating with emotion. She drew from her girdle a shining blade of obsidian in an ivory handle. "Stand aside while I remove that devil's poison, and if you don't want me to take this knife to the shooter's throat, get him away. I'll see to Shamus."

Beth gave the little man one last peck on the cheek, and let John draw her up. She cried out, for though not seriously injured, she carried shot from her father's gun at several places in her body. She realized blood trickled down her face.

"Let her kill him," John exclaimed, swinging her up into his arms. "I must see to you."

Beth shook her head. "My injuries are not life-threatening. If my father is found here with his throat slit, it will cause more trouble than he is worth."

Just then a tall, muscular man stumbled into the clearing from the wood. It was Murphy, blood streaming down his head. He surveyed the scene. "I wasn't in time, then. I called out a warning. I didn't know exactly where you'd be, nor can I find my way about in these woods as easily as Lord Blayne can." He approached Blayne and leaned over, touching his neck. "Still alive.

A pity. I'll take charge of him, my lord, while you see to your lady."

Murphy appeared not to see the faery queen or Shamus. He picked up Lord Blayne. Hoisting him over his shoulder, Murphy carried him off through the woods toward Blayne Manor.

Beth refused to let John carry her away from the scene until she knew the outcome of the surgery on Shamus. The faery queen made quick work of the small ball of lead on his forehead. Then she cut away his clothing and looked at the wound in his neck.

"A more dangerous spot," Beth murmured, coming up beside her.

"In more ways than one. The ball lies deep. To cut there is to risk damaging his muscles. Not to cut is to let that poison destroy him all the faster." The queen did not look at Beth as she spoke. Her knife was already probing the wound. Shamus moaned and struggled. Beth put her hands on his shoulders to hold him still, while John gently but firmly restrained his torso and legs.

The moments seemed like hours; the blood seemed more than such a small body could spare, but at last the queen gave a gurgle in her own language that needed no translation, for it was pure triumph. She flipped out the lead, then stood. "Not a moment to waste. Shamus must come with me to faery. Mrs. Longford, you come too. I'll tend your wounds there. You are going to have some scars if you stay here. Will your handsome young man still want you then?"

John pulled Beth up and held her possessively against him. "She stays here."

"Very well, then. Use this. She will heal faster." She held out the knife to him, and he took it. "May we meet again." And she disappeared in an eyeblink, taking Shamus with her.

John lifted Beth into his arms and began striding across the meadow to the village gate, to which he carried the key. The quickest way to her cottage would be down her carriageway. "Is there a local physician?"

She shook her head. "You'll have to do it. Will I be very ugly?"

He kissed the two places, one on her temple and one on her cheek, that bled sluggishly. "You'll always be the most beautiful woman in the world to me, no matter what."

Chapter 18

It would have been too much to expect that the sound of a shotgun at dawn, following several episodes of ethereal music, would not have attracted attention. As John started down the path to Hintock cottage, he was met by his coachman and Beth's maid. Behind them, at the village gate to St. Anne's Well, voices of villagers could be heard, and the gate rattled. John heard the voice of the vicar saying he had the key. Others warned him that they must go to Lord Blayne for permission.

John had no time for them, or Blayne, or anything else. He hastened to the cottage and carried Beth upstairs. Mavis, frightened but surprisingly calm, undressed her. It was found that wherever she was clothed, no piece of shot had done more than barely pierce the skin. The balls were easily removed, and Mavis did it with tweezers. She sent the fluttering, half-hysterical Mrs. Pettistone downstairs to brew a poultice to stem the bleeding and clean the wounds. John stood by, refusing to leave. This forced Mavis to manipulate a sheet this way and that to protect her mistress's privacy. At last the wounds on her head had to be addressed, and Mavis looked worriedly at them. There, the balls had sunk out of sight, though the oozing wounds and swellings told their whereabouts.

"I don't know, m'lord. I've never cut into anyone before." Mavis's hands were shaking.

"John can do it," Beth said confidently. "It would be quite unusual for a man who has spent many years shooting birds and been to war not to have had to remove bullets and shot before."

In spite of himself, John found his hands a little shaky too. *I've removed shot from friends on the hunting field, but I never had a care for what the results would look like afterward,* he thought. But he did not wish to voice such a concern to Beth, for fear any scars created would bother her more than they need.

"Slip a nightgown on her, and I'll see what I can do," he told Mavis. "Is there any laudanum in the house?"

"Do you think me a coward, then?" Beth challenged him, chin up.

"No, I think you too brave for your own good. The less it hurts, the less likely you are to jerk and make me cut too deeply. It is the sewing them up after that concerns me. You'd best do that, Mavis."

Mrs. Pettistone had returned by this time to assure them that the poultice was being brewed by the cook and would be brought up soon. Timidly she stepped forward.

"If it please your lordship," she said, "I am accounted one of the finest seamstresses in this part of the country."

"That she is," Beth said, and Mavis nodded agreement.

"Much better than me, m'lord," the usually redoubtable maid said with a slight quaver to her voice. "And you *will* take laudanum, Mrs. Longford!" She bustled from the room and returned moments later with a small vial, and made Beth drink from it.

So, using the knife that the faery queen had given him, which he found was sharper and made a thinner cut than any he had ever before used, he carefully probed the raised wounds until he felt the lead shot embedded there. Then, with the point of the knife, he gently pried them out. Neither cut was very deep or long. Beth lay quietly under his ministrations, and he held her hand while Mrs. Pettistone stitched her up, jabbering as she did so about how she would use silk thread in a loop stitch that could easily be removed as the wound healed.

He could tell by the little twitches in Beth's hand that the sewing was painful, perhaps more so than the removal of the shot had been, but she lay quietly, letting Mrs. Pettistone do her work. The stitches did, indeed, look neat to him. By the time they were set, the poultice had arrived, and he retreated to let the women administer to Beth's wounds.

He found waiting for him in the hall outside both the vicar and one of the local magistrates, a man of his own age named Harold Osbald. The latter, after enquiring into Beth's welfare, asked John to come downstairs to explain what had happened in the meadow that night.

"You should know, my lord, that Lord Blayne has lodged a complaint against you for attempting to rape his daughter, and claims he shot at you, hitting her by mistake. He also says you had a confederate, a Mr. Murphy, who dragged him away and tied him up before he could even learn if she was harmed. He also accuses you of kidnaping his wife."

"So Lord Blayne is deeply concerned about his daughter, eh? Why is he not here right now instead of you?"

"He was badly roughed up by that Irishman, and has taken to his bed."

"Ha! He is afraid to come near here. I might decide to return his compliment! Certainly he must know I would not permit him near her ever again."

Osbald eyed him carefully. "Perhaps it would be best if you told me what happened in your own words."

"Perhaps I should wait and let Mrs. Longforth tell you who has injured her, and who has protected her from worse injury. But I should warn you, Mr. Osbald, that Lord Blayne has been showing signs of mental instability for some time now. He has attempted the murder of his wife, which is why I sent her into hiding."

Harold looked torn by these words. "I must have confirmation of this. When will Mrs. Longford be able to see me?"

"She took laudanum while her wounds were being stitched, so I am not sure when she will feel like talking. In the meantime, I demand that Lord Blayne be arrested and securely held, lest he attempt to attack her, or someone else, again."

"Meaning you. If you attempted to rape his daughter, he would be justified..."

"Mr. Osbald, I know you have been a neighbor and friend of Blayne's for many years..."

"That will not prejudice me, my lord, but such charges must be investigated."

"I will check on Mrs. Longford to see when she thinks she will be able to speak with you."

"I would prefer you to remain with me. I do not wish her to be intimidated," Osbald objected, but John turned on his heel and hastened up the stairs. Entering Beth's room, he ignored Mavis's shushing noise and gently shook Beth awake. Quickly he informed her of her father's charge.

"We cannot tell the truth, any more than he can," she murmured sleepily.

"No, but we can say he objected to our plans to marry."

Beth nodded. "He shot me to prevent it, before you could interpose yourself to protect me."

"That fits your wounds quite well. What sort of a man is Osbald?"

"A persistent one. He has proposed to me once a fortnight for the last two years."

John groaned. All he needed was for the local magistrate to be a jealous suitor.

"I am sending for those doctors now. We must see that your father is confined. I take it that you would prefer that to a criminal trial?"

Beth nodded, her mouth a grim line.

"Until then, I must somehow see that your father is locked up. You rest."

Beth tried to sit up. "How can I, not knowing whether he will try to kill you on sight?"

"I can say the same of you. I only hope your persistent suitor does not take it in his head to lock me up instead of your father."

"Let me speak with Osbald. I think I can convince him to take my father into custody."

"Very well."

John brought Osbald up. Beth sat propped up on the side on which there were fewer wounds. The poultice had been removed; her stitches were prominent. Osbald gasped as he saw her.

"Mrs. Longford! Your beautiful face! Tell me what happened."

Beth drew breath, but Osbald held up his hand. "Without Lord Wayneathe's presence, if you please. I want to be sure you tell the truth without being afraid of his bullying. If he tries to force you to lie, I will, I assure you, act on your behalf."

"It is not he I need protection from. Lord Wayneathe, you may go. Mavis will stay, and anyway, I am quite safe with Mr. Osbald."

Once John had gone, Beth motioned the magistrate into a chair by her bed. "The tale is quickly told, Mr. Osbald. My father shot me. I don't know why, exactly. I just saw him running toward us with a shotgun and before John could prevent him, he fired directly at me. I think he is mad, sir."

"I would be rather angry myself, to find my daughter in a meadow in the dark of night with a man not her husband," Osbald said, looking very offended.

"I did not mean angry. I meant mad. As in having lost his reason."

"Why were you alone with Lord Wayneathe in the

meadow at night? Not proper, not proper at all. Any father would object."

"Enough to shoot his daughter? As to why we were there, like many others in the area, we were awakened by strange sounds."

"Ah, yes, the vicar and several others told me of that. What sort of sounds?"

"Music. Ethereal music. I have no idea what caused it. It sounded as if it came from St. Anne's Well. We walked over there to try to discover the cause, but it had ceased by the time we got there. We were standing there speculating on the source of the music when my father charged out at us."

"Hmmm. Well, his actions could have resulted from misinterpreting what he saw."

"What did he claim to see that would justify shooting me, pray tell?"

"That Wayneathe was attempting to rape you."

"Never! John would not do such a thing, and no such mistake could have been made. Wayneathe was several feet from me when father charged, firing his shotgun."

"But why would he do such a thing?"

"Perhaps to prevent me from marrying Wayneathe. Not exactly sane behavior, I am sure you will agree."

Osbald drew in a deep breath. "Do you mean to marry Wayneathe?"

"Yes, I do. Now, do you think it sane for a father to object to such a match? Even if I were underage, instead of a widow in her mid-twenties, to shoot me, or him, for such a reason is the act of a madman."

"You are wounded on your side, as well as your face. It was Lord Wayneathe your father meant to shoot. You in fact jumped in front of your lover to protect him."

"And if I did? My father had no justification for firing at either of us. I demand that you arrest him for assault."

Osbald rubbed his chin. "This puts me in a very peculiar position. Lord Blayne is an old friend. You are a woman I deeply admire. Lord Wayneathe is a known libertine, under whose influence you have fallen. Perhaps . . ."

"Perhaps you would like to announce to father that I am engaged to you?"

Osbald opened his eyes wide.

"But you have always refused me. And you just said . . ."

"I refuse you still. I am asking if you would trust my father to accept such an announcement with complacency. He told me once, after the first time I refused you, that I did well to do so, that he would kill you before he would see me married to one so much beneath me."

Osbald turned purple. "He said that?"

"As God is my witness. If you doubt me, ask my mother. Now, shall I announce to him that we are to be wed?"

Osbald turned pale, and sweat popped out on his forehead. "He is indeed unpredictable and of a dangerous temperament. I begin to see what you mean. I will get some men and arrest him, if you swear to me, and will swear under oath, that the attack was unprovoked, and was not in any way an attempt to protect you."

"I will swear to that with a clear conscience."

"Very well. I will arrest him and see that he is confined until this matter is thoroughly examined."

Beth nearly went mad herself waiting for John to return with word about her father. Morning passed into afternoon before he at last mounted the steps to her room. He looked grim, and held in his hand a sealed missive.

"What has happened, John?"

He sat on the side of the bed and drew her into his arms. She could not help but wince, for some of her wounds were beginning to hurt.

"My poor darling. I am sorry." He loosened his hold. "Sorry for so many things. I hardly know if this will be good news or bad for you."

"Tell me!"

"When we went to Blayne Manor, the servants were all terrified. They said your father had barricaded himself in the smoking room and fired shots out the window at anyone who came within his view. Likewise, he fired at the door when anyone approached it. Smithson has some facial lacerations from splinters to repay his faithful service."

"Oh, no!"

"We attempted to reason with him, but he shot at us in the same manner from the windows and the door, which he in fact opened so he could see down the stairs and cut down anyone who attempted to climb them. He was getting drunker and drunker, of course, so I hoped he would eventually pass out and we could go up and arrest him.

"About an hour ago, we heard a single shot, from a pistol. Then nothing. I decided to venture up a ladder to take a look in the windows. I saw him slumped over his desk."

"He shot himself." Beth's expression told John little about her feelings. She fell back against the pillow.

"Yes. He was dead. Surrounded by gold coins. I expect half of the £5000 was there, strewn about."

"Half?" Beth focused on the details, to avoid the full realization of her father's death.

"Shamus *said* Murphy was an honest Irishman. Apparently he took only his share of Shamus's gold."

Beth turned her head to one side, and John said nothing, waiting for her to digest what he had told her. He doubted she would mourn her father, but the news must still be a shock to her.

At last she turned back. "I think it was for the best. He would have hated being confined." And she began to weep. He held her and rocked her like a baby until she had cried herself out. At last she lifted her head from his shoulder. "What is that?"

John fingered the piece of paper nervously.

Beth looked at the letter in his hand. "For me? From father?"

"Yes. There was one for your mother, too. Perhaps you should wait until you are stronger to read it."

"No." She took it as if she had been handed something nasty, though, and held it for a long while before opening it.

Tears began running down her cheeks. Wordlessly, she held it out to John. "You read it. I can't make it out."

"It is an apology to you, and an admission of guilt. He makes no mention of Shamus. He says Terry joined the army not to emulate me, but because he loathed his father for his treatment of you and his mother, and for bankrupting the estate. Terry couldn't bear to be around him, and hoped he would die in battle."

Beth began to sob out loud. "I felt it. When Terry said goodbye before leaving for the continent, it seemed to be a final farewell."

"We can't show this letter to the authorities. Not if you want him buried in consecrated ground."

"You mean because it shows he was probably in his right mind at the end?"

"I'm afraid so."

"It should matter to me, shouldn't it, John? Where he is buried, I mean. But it just doesn't. I feel no forgiveness in my heart for him. I suppose that means I'll never be forgiven my sins."

John shook his head. "You will forgive him some day. Forgiving and forgetting are two different things. You must know he wasn't in his right mind that evening when he gambled away his daughter. Perhaps even as long ago as when you were five and he seduced your governess, leaving you to wander the woods unattended. Even then, he conducted his affairs like a madman, my father always used to say."

Beth sighed and snuggled deeper into John's arms. "I hope you are right. I would like to be rid of this burden of anger and hate and—yes—guilt. I've long wondered if I should have done the dutiful thing and married Lord Bannermain as he wished. If perhaps that wouldn't have set him right and he wouldn't have left Terry's inheritance in such straits, and . . ."

"Bosh! He was what he was. He would have gone on the same way no matter whom you married. Guilt! Like hatred, it is a corrosive emotion. My guilt over Terry's death caused me to live in so indecent, so despicable a manner that it almost cost me the love of my life."

"Oh, John." Beth lifted her head, and he met her lips with his in a kiss that went from comforting to sizzling in seconds. At which point they heard a loud *harrumph*, and turned to see that Mavis had not given up her chair by the fire, and was staring at them quite indignantly.

John growled. "We'd best be married soon, love. I can't take much more of that face glaring at me." Then he bent down to whisper in her ear. "I think this means you have thought through what I told you about the differences between Longford's kisses and mine?"

She looked troubled, and John felt his heart stutter in his chest.

"It won't be the same, Beth. One thing a reformed rake can offer you is knowledge of how to please a woman, knowledge your first husband lacked or did not wish to use."

"I hope you are right. I do not wish to be a disappointment to you."

"I am right!" He kissed her once more, tenderly.

Beth felt heat coursing through her veins, and knew he told the truth. "Yes, we will marry soon. Quietly, by license, of course. But soon. I'll not put off our wedding for my father; to mourn him to that extent would be hypocrisy."

Another kiss told of John's complete agreement.

Mavis's objection caused Beth to pull away.

"Throw this on the fire, will you, John?" She handed

him her father's note. He complied, his expression approving.

"Did we save Shamus? We don't really know if his wounds were fatal or not."

John frowned. "I feel sure that we did. Once in faery, he will heal, surely."

"I pray so. Perhaps someday he will send us a message, somehow."

Epilogue

The Heartwood, June 1819

Beth and John crept silently through the Heartwood, feeling like naughty children who had escaped their tutor. The men from the Linnean Society who had come to study the flora and fauna of the Heartwood had gone at last, and they could have the place, and one another, to themselves.

John, holding a substantial picnic basket in one hand, kept the other protectively under Beth's arm at all times, mindful of her interesting condition. She looked at him with a mixture of adoration and annoyance, for in her fifth month, she could hardly be considered delicate.

At last they reached Grandfather Tree, and settled down by the Princess Stone. Beth began lifting items out of the basket while John spread the picnic cloth and cutlery. When they had finished these tasks, they paused as one to look around the clearing, and simultaneous sighs came from each.

"Do you think he lived?"

John cupped Beth's cheek and answered the question as he had dozens of times before. "I am sure he did."

"Will we ever see him again?" She did not expect an answer, nor did he have one for her. They leaned into one another and shared a kiss.

Later, Beth thought, her blood pumping languorous warmth through her body. *Later we will make love.* She longed to do so right there under the oak tree, but they never had, not for fear of human discovery so much as that of an unseen visitor from faery.

"I am pleased that Sir James Smith was able to confirm the trout in the pool as a new subspecies," John commented.

Beth beamed at him over her full plate. "And the dragonfly! That was an especially sweet victory, since Professor MacDuff had been so sure that my drawing was inaccurate!"

"He knows better now!" John looked fierce. "There is no finer wildlife artist than you in Britain. I intend to see your drawings published so all can know it."

At that moment an acorn fell, bouncing from John's head with surprising velocity. He looked up into the thick leaves of the old tree suspiciously.

"Should you, I wonder?" Beth mused, picking up the acorn and turning it over in her hand. "It would bring notice to the place, and more visitors."

"We would still have approval on who visits here and who does not." Another acorn whacked John, this time a glancing blow from the side. He cocked his head, and then grinned. "In fact, we should consider holding an open house here several times a year."

Abruptly the two were pelted with acorns. They seemed to come from every side.

Beth looked at John in wonderment. "I have never known an acorn to fall from the side," she exclaimed.

"I have!" John stood up. "Show yourself, you old rascal."

Strange musical notes filled the air around them, and it was clear to both that more than one voice was involved.

"Shamus! Have you brought Bedelia? Please come out!"

High above them, a wizened face peeped through the leaves. "She's a bit shy. And fearful for the young ones."

"Oh!" Beth clapped her hands together. "You've brought them, too!"

"Aye." He disappeared, then reappeared moments later from the other side of the tree. He hesitated, studying the two carefully for a moment. "You're happy, then."

"Very." Beth smiled, tears trembling in her eyes. "And you?"

"'Tis pure bliss, with my beloved mate and my troop of youngsters. The haven you've made for us and other creatures of faery on your Irish estates is appreciated, my lord."

"You live there, then? We've visited twice, and never seen any sign . . ."

"No. Though Mr. Murphy is a most protective caretaker, we spend most of our time in faery, for the sake of the children's safety. We just visit from time to time, to pick mushrooms." Shamus drew closer. "Are those seed cakes, by any chance? The children loved the ones you left for us."

Beth held out the basket of seed cakes, and Shamus stepped forward tentatively, eyeing John.

"Not afraid of me, are you? Not now?"

"Just out of practice, you might say. What nonsense is this about opening the Heartwood? How can we come here when there are people all over? Who was that pompous fellow you brought here yesterday?"

"If I had known you were here, I would have sent him right away," Beth declared, and reached out for Shamus, who went into her arms for a hug. Then he threw his head back, and a long, joyful burble of sound came out. The nearest tree branch began to shake and shimmer, and suddenly three little heads peeped out, and one larger one, her features anxiously fixed on John.

Beth and John stared back, surprised to find that the

little leprechauns looked as wizened as their parents, and wore the same weathered coats that looked like lichen.

John stood up. "At last I have the opportunity to apologize to you, madam, for frightening you when I was a child."

The female leprechaun smiled tentatively, revealing canine teeth markedly sharper than her mate's. "I thought you might still be angry with me for biting you."

"Not at all. Self-defense."

Shamus by this time had made his way up the tree trunk, and carried the basket of seed cakes over to his family. "We can't stay long," he said. "But I had to bring you this gift."

So saying, he dropped a small leather pouch to the ground and watched, grinning, as John picked it up.

A sudden chorus of sounds rose from the little leprechauns.

"Quite right, my children. Give it to Beth to open, John. Now, wave goodbye, my children, to your true friends among the sons of man."

The small hands fluttered, and then the trio disappeared into the foliage, followed by their mother. A few seconds later the now-empty basket wafted down to the ground. Shamus stayed behind, eyes on the leather pouch.

"Go ahead, open it."

Beth pulled on the drawstring and opened the pouch. Reaching inside, she brought out a pair of exquisitely made baby shoes in a pale pink shade.

"Oh, Shamus! They are lovely." Beth held them to her heart. "The most beautiful shoes in the world! Does the color tell us you know something we don't?"

"You may thank the faery queen for that knowledge. Divination is not among the leprechaun's gifts. Look some more, my dear."

Beth, eyes wide, dipped her hand into the pouch again as John held up the little pink shoes for close inspection.

"Magnificent," he said, looking up at Shamus with a grin, only to discover that the leprechaun had disappeared.

Just then, Beth gasped.

"What is it?" John hastily knelt beside her, and she held up a second pair of little shoes, of pale blue.

SIGNET

REGENCY ROMANCE
Now Available

Winter Dreams
by Sandra Heath

Judith Callard's twin brother is in trouble, so she follows Lord Penventon—the man responsible—into one of Lisbon's seedier districts. What she finds there inflames her jealousy and puts her life in danger.

0-451-21236-3

The Harem Bride
by Blair Bancroft

Jason Lisbourne can seduce any woman he wants, but he can't dislodge the hold Penelope Blayne has on his soul. Now he has a chance to be her knight in shining armor, unless pride—and a secret—get in the way.

0-451-21006-9

Available wherever books are sold, or
to order call: 1-800-788-6262

Signet Regency Romance from
Amanda McCabe

One Touch of Magic	0-451-20936-2
A Loving Spirit	0-451-20801-3
The Golden Feather	0-451-20728-8
The Errant Earl	0-451-20629-0
Lady Rogue	0-451-20521-9
The Spanish Bride	0-451-20401-8

Available wherever books are sold or to order call 1-800-788-6262

S057

Allison Lane

"A FORMIDABLE TALENT...
MS. LANE NEVER FAILS TO
DELIVER THE GOODS."
—*ROMANTIC TIMES*

BIRDS OF A FEATHER
0-451-19825-5
When a plain, bespectacled young woman keeps meeting the handsome Lord Wylie, she feels she is not up to his caliber. A great arbiter of fashion for London society, Lord Wylie was reputed to be more interested in the cut of his clothes than the feelings of others, as the young woman bore witness to. Degraded by him in public, she could nevertheless not forget his dashing demeanor. It will take a public scandal, and a private passion, to bring them together...

Available wherever books are sold or
to order call: 1-800-788-6262